SHADOW

In The Bridge World

MIKE DORN WISS

For my Zaida, Henry Lehrer
A century young
A lucky cardholder

Thanks to Phred Gitelman for hand analyses and
Caroline for the burr under my saddle.

CLAIMER
Any resemblance to characters living or dead is
probably intentional and not likely coincidental.
Any litigation should be directed to the author's
attorney, bearing in mind the difficulties inherent
in getting blood from stones.
MDW

Published by JBF Press
Box 229, 1450 Johnston Road, White Rock, B.C. V4B 5E9

ISBN 0–9697213–0–7

Table of Contents

* *Previously published in slightly different form in the Ontario KIBITZER, and reprinted with permission of the editor.*

Introduction

IF YOU WERE TO ASK, I WOULDN'T GIVE you a straight answer. If I gave you a straight answer, it would probably be a lie. Perhaps that sounds as if I were running for office. In reality, I'm simply protecting the privacy of a friend.

I've known Alan (which is the name I'm going to give him; if I were you I wouldn't bet the farm it's his real one) since we were frosh at the University of Saskatchewan. We had actually met two years previous while playing golf in a high school tournament, where I'd beaten him for the first (and last) time in my life, but it wasn't until we shared classes in university that we became close friends. He had had the good fortune to have been born with a platinum spoon for every orifice, and parents who, as he grew, never let the realisation that he was more advantaged than his peers go to his head. Even were he born broke, he was blessed with brains the least humble Mensian would have envied (only a slight exaggeration), and as he matured, physical attributes that let him excel at the many sports he enjoyed.

We remained in touch the following year when I moved to the Twin Cities in naive pursuit of a young model whose legs began somewhere in the vicinity of her ears. While I was stupidly off eloping in Escanaba, he was suffering the tragedy of losing both his parents to an accident, one of simply being in the wrong place at the wrong time. He was forced to drop out of school to raise his sister, and take over the responsibility of a business that was growing faster than a culture of bacteria.

It wasn't too many years before his sister was out of high school and into college, college boys, and the illusion of independence. Alan sold the business, and simply retired. Rich, healthy, young, and possessing all the time in the world, he devoted himself to sport, and the sports that he loved. Golf and tennis and badminton; sailing, surfing, and soaring; curling and bowling; chess and bridge and 'go'. Individual and intellectual sports were his choices, those where he could fail or succeed, and sometimes excel, alone. Those where he could be responsible only for his own performance.

The unique, the amazing thing about Alan is that he is known and recognised as an expert in each sport and by every peer.

He's won two pro golf tournaments, a PBA bowling title, a bronze medal in the '68 Winter Olympics, a state chess tourney, a dozen regionals (and a national) at bridge, beaten Laver at tennis in Australia, Trevino in a ten dollar Nassau in Albuquerque...the list goes on.

Now if you've been paying attention you'll be wondering why you haven't heard of this man, why this incredible real-life Plimpton (*with* talent) hasn't been heralded on network television or the covers of national magazines.

Simple, really. Alan abhors publicity, and actively shuns it by the use of one of the many skills he has mastered... the art of disguise.

Three weeks under the tutelage of one of Hollywood's top makeup artists, months of practice, the gift of mimicry, and a knack for picking great names out of telephone books have kept Alan invisible as he plays his personal game of hopscotch between sports. You know him, but you don't know him.

Like a Shadow he slips silently from sport to sport, seen but unrecognised, recognised but unknown, altering his name and appearance, his dress and demeanor, to succeed and survive in the social strata that layer each sport. Anonymity, after all, is the key to the survival of his lifestyle. To remove its cloak and bare not only his many accomplishments, but also his wealth and the looks to turn the head of any lady under eighty, or perhaps just any one under the stars, and what you have is not anonymity. What you have is the cover of People magazine.

* * *

"So," the Shadow asked me, "what do you see as the *essence* of the sport? Surely not winning..."

"No?" I teased.

"No. Nor its resultant end products, whether they be money, prestige, or, perish the thought, monkey points. If you were that interested in winning, you'd be playing on teams where you were the worst player, not doing just the opposite." He lifted his shot of Glenfiddich to his lips, sipped at it while he studied me from under his brow. I remained obstinately silent; such questions were usually rhetorical. "Perhaps," he went on, "it's the competitive or the social aspects. Bridge isn't unique in its ability to combine the two, although it certainly does it in a unique manner. Maybe, Mikey," he poked, "you play it only for fun, as a game, a pastime, and not as a sport."

"Perish *that* thought," I said. The Shadow smiled.

"I didn't mean it to appear as if I were chiding you." He chuckled and placed his glass carefully on the centre of his napkin.

I rarely give serious thought to such comments, from anybody. In the Shadow's case they are merely indicative of his sensitivity and honest concern for the feelings of others. Empathy is not a word foreign to his vocabulary. But when it comes to his friends, and also to the odd friendly acquaintance, he is forever deriving entertainment from verbal pokes that skirt the edges of fair play, or occasionally even good taste; conscious and constant comments designed to test, to define one's everchanging states of being through his personal interpretations of reactions to his proddings. I cunningly counter this foible by simply refusing to react. I therefore stared at him blankly, and waited.

Tiring of my patience, he picked up his scotch and tossed it back in a single motion. "Let me put it another way," he said. "What is the essence of bridge that makes it such a poignant microcosm of life?" He looked directly into my eyes. It was like staring through Paul Newman's baby blues into the soul of Rasputin.

"This isn't one of your typical philosophical discourses in barroom drivel, is it? You really *do* want an answer."

"I run my life by the answer," he said, " and you are my friend. What you think *is* important to me."

*   *   *

Well,'Alan', it has taken me fifteen years to give you my answer. And since bridge, like life, is a composition of infinite variety, any answer can be only partial, and forever incomplete.

I hope you dig it, good buddy...

Shadow Cruising

I LOST THREE DAYS OF THE HAWAII Regional at a Thanksgiving luau in Lahaina. It was the New Year, of course, and not Thanksgiving, but then we were luauing a turkey, not a porker, and we were giving thanks to the camaraderie that brought us together, not toasting a time of year that in Hawaii is very much like any other time of year.

The turkey was decorated with slabs of yam and chunks of pineapple the size of a preschooler's fist, and was served with papaya punch and a salad decorated with thin strips of avocado and smothered with special Hana mushrooms. Shared with good company the combination was too strong for even the pull of bridge to budge.

A courtesy call to the Shadow's hotel room in Honolulu changed all that.

"Wiss, you jerk! I've been looking for you for two days. Where the hell are you?"

"Lahaina. Still enjoying the leftovers of a luau with some friends."

"Well, grab the first flight out of Kapalua and get your ass over here. You're working."

"Working?"

In those halcyon days of owning fewer than four digits of ACBL attendance/participaction/reward points I was sometimes in demand as a minor pro, being somewhat of a minor expert. Now that I must admit to possessing at least one fractional over the magic minimum of the day I am less in demand, being a minor expert still.

"I got you a client for the Bee Open."

"No kidding?"

"Fifty a session; not great."

"Less your personal agent's fee?"

"A mere seventy-five percent, but if you do well there's a helluva bonus."

"Client is a tall and foxy redhead?"

"More like Methuselah's granduncle."

"*That's* graphic. Must be some bonus."

"How about an island cruise? He and his cronies have chartered a boat, Honolulu to Kailua-Kona, nickel rubber and good food and drink all the way. All you have to do to get in is not offend him, which in your case, I'll admit, is not a trivial request. Do well and you may get to wear the Cap'n's cap."

"Sounds great. What's he like?"

"One of the nicest old gents you'll ever meet. Reminds me of Otto Leesment."

"Otto? I've played with Otto, numerous times, back when I was a thirty-year-old rookie."

"Yes," the Shadow drawled, "he *was* a patient fellow. So's Francis here, but other than that and a physical resemblance the similarities end there. His doc banished him to a wheelchair fifteen years ago, so he changed docs. Still walks with two canes. (Great, a thought flashed insanely, north-south both sessions!) Says he'll climb in his grave before he climbs in a wheelchair."

"Sounds like he might get notrumps in before me a bit too often."

"Maybe. He can be stubborn all right, but he's not a bad player. He didn't take the game up until he was seventy and he's determined to get his gold card before he croaks."

"No kidding? That's great. Think he'll make it?"

There was a slight pause on the line. "Maybe," Alan said again.

* * *

Francis was a kindly old gent, just as the Shadow had said. Some people that age get cranky, mostly because of aches and pains, and some get downright bitter, mostly because they haven't dealt with mortality or are pissed off at themselves that they didn't do it sooner, but my bridge partner of the day was not of either ilk. Rather he revelled in life, not seeming to care if he had a minute left or a decade. The card gods seem to favour such people. He kept raising me on wings and prayers and his angels kept coming home on both.

Twice the opponents misdefended double-dummy to hand us unmakeable contracts, both played from the wrong side - mine. Three times he bid non-suits in an effort to get me to play the hand, each time for an average or better result. The odds began to catch up with us midway through the session, but that was just about the time I began to smarten up and underbid my hands by a queen or so. We finally meandered in with a 209 and Francis had four goldies for his section top and ten years more youth in each leg as we headed for a light dinner.

"Know something?" he said over a salad, "I was kinda testing you this afternoon. I coulda bit notrumps a few times but I wanted to see how you handled some tough ones. Didn't expect us to do so well, actually. We had luck, didn't we?"

"Yessir. Quite a bit." I smiled and shrugged.

"You call me Francis. Tell me... what do you think of my game?"

"Well...Francis, you don't do anything great, but more importantly, you don't do anything really bad. One of the marks of a good player is consistency, and those making the fewest mistakes do best. Your tempo's pretty good, but it'd be better if you thought in advance what card an opponent might play to give you a problem. Your concentration is real good. I could learn from you in that department."

"Thanks. You expect we'll do well tonight?"

"I can't kid you, Francis, I doubt it. The opponents were more than friendly, and this isn't a playthrough."

"Be honest with me; how can I improve my game?"

I cleared my throat, giving myself time to clear my mind before saying anything I might regret, or, more likely, phrasing something in a regretful manner. "Before you bid, Francis, most especially on hands of a balanced nature, take the nearest king in your hand and mentally eat it. The scoring system rewards aggression, but you're taking it way too far. Your card play is pretty darn good; you shouldn't be steering hands in my direction when you know they'll play better from your side. Try to have the hand played from whatever side warrants it. Also, it would help you a lot if you learned a few simple defensive aids. You seem to do all right naturally in guessing situations in the middle of the hand, but some of these aren't guesses at all, and in those cases you'll be able to gain."

He grinned at me. "Let you in on something," he said. "I'm apt as not to fall asleep before the fourth round. Never been more than a board over in a second session in my life. Just too damn old. If it's all the same to you, I'd as soon not play tonight. Rather sit around over brandies and talk some bridge and get to bed early."

"Fine with me, Francis."

"And I appreciate the criticism. You say some of the same things Alan does. By the way, I'd like you both to accompany me and some friends on a cruise Monday. He mention it to you?"

Thinking fast is an attribute I've always kept handy in a pocket somewhere in my mind. Trouble is, I occasionally forget which pocket. How in hell did Francis know the Shadow by his real name? In the bridge world he always went by (censored). And why did an old man who wanted goldies not want a fair chance at more holding a healthy carryover into the final?

"Uh, he mentioned the possibility of it," I stammered, another tempo-gaining ploy. "He asked me if I could make it, if you wanted to invite me, that is."

"I do." He stabbed a tomato chunk and shook it at me as a means of emphasis. "You young fellows remind me of me, before I got responsible and settled down to make some money." He chuckled and chomped on the tomato. "Now that I'm irresponsible again I enjoy the company of more agile minds. Some of my friends are getting a bit on the doddery side, if you catch my connotation."

"These friends be on the cruise?" I ventured safely.

"Every last one of them. Getting to be a tradition with us the first Monday after the regional. Good balm for a thousand ills. And rubber is a happy rest from the tension of matchpoints."

"You've noticed that, too?"

"Yup. Known these folks a long time. Learned the game from them. They just never got the duplicate bug; never had a chance to, really. That virus I got from Alan."

"Uh, Alan started you on duplicate? He never mentioned it to me." Wounded, to the quick.

"No? Well, it's a long story. I can see why he might not have brought it up. Maybe we'll get to it when we're aboard, after you've had a chance to meet my friends."

                              *   *   *

Matchpoints has always tended to fry my brain, as have most matchpoint opponents. Raised in the never-neverland where rhyme and reason have little solid footing, results are all that count. For this reason I tend to avoid pairs games and gravitate towards teams, where the play retains a certain grace and a respect for finer elements found mostly in IMP and rubber bridge. Knockouts are a favourite form of the game, but unfortunately many of them suffer from inhuman starting times. Normally I look forward to the Sunday Swiss events which end each tournament.

On this Sunday, however, I could feel I wasn't right, which wasn't difficult, since I knew what was wrong. I was too busy looking forward to Monday. My sleep had been stirred with dreams of anticipation of the cruise. I was a little tired and I knew my concentration would be off. I was playing on a team with two friends from California and another from Minnesota, the kind of team that rated to finish six and two, and win maybe one time in thirty. Today make that forty.

In spite of my play we were three and a quarter at the half. Francis had piqued my curiosity the day before, impressing me with his wit and charm and wisdom, all stirred in the elixir of longevity. When I should have been concentrating on the vulnerable notrump game I was in, my mind drifted to a tomorrow with Francis and me on the bow of a ship in the channel, discussing the many things we'd only touched on the evening before. I counted my tricks hastily, saw ten if a suit broke favourably, and failed to take a simple safety play for nine in case it didn't. As luck would have it, the suit broke anyway, but partner's raised eyebrows and my own carelessness shook me up enough to seek out the Shadow at halftime.

He found me first.

"Drop your pakalolo, Bra'?" a voice said behind me. I whirled to stare into Alan's grinning face.

"Jeez, don't do that," I breathed, clutching my chest. "My pacemaker's in the shop for repairs."

"How're you doing?"

"The team's a lucky three and a quarter, but I'm playing lousy. You?"

"We've lost one. The client's played great all four matches but her partner blew one trying to play better than she was. What's your problem?"

"Just concentration. Been thinking about your friend Francis, looking forward to tomorrow more than playing today."

Alan smiled. "I see. I had an early breakfast with him today. He likes you. Nice result yesterday, by the way."

"Thanks. Yeah, I like him, too. He lets out just enough of himself to let you know there's a lot more there."

"Not like his bidding."

"Not like his bidding." I grinned.

"Well, stem your curiousities till the morning, when all will be revealed. I have to go; dinner with the team and all that. If I miss you later meet me and Francis for coffee after sunrise. We're having breakfast on board later; you'll meet the rest of the gang - and I do mean gang - then. Later." He squeezed my arm and turned to leave. As he was rounding the nearest corner he tossed over his shoulder, "Good luck tonight. If you play the Hog chew off his curly pink tail for me, will you?" And he was gone.

*   *   *

Morning could have come no slower for me. By sunrise I was already on the beach, having nursed a number through the predawn starlight. By the time Alan and Francis arrived on the patio of the coffee shop I was already halfway through a pot of Kona. Good mornings chorused over the clatter of fresh cups and saucers brought by an attentive waitress.

"Did you do better last night?" Alan asked.

"Yes, thanks. The whole team played well. We got beat by two better teams. You?"

"Nothing new; six and two. I rather hoped we'd meet you in the evening."

"Unlucky." I turned to Francis. "Sorry I missed you yesterday. You didn't play, did you?"

"No, I was getting things ready for today. Kibitzed Alan's first match in the evening and got to bed early. There was a great hand; tell him, Alan."

"Six no, but there's a tune-up to the tale. When we arrived at the table our opponents, a pretty ancient pair, were already there, making the boards. Wifey was telling hubby not to worry about how crazy the opponents bid and just to lead fourth best. *She* always did and it usually worked. So on the first hand out of the chute partner and I had three or four misunderstandings in the auction and got to the notrump slam on these wonderful cards..." Alan scribbled quickly on a napkin.

PARTNER (THE DUMMY)
♠ x x x
♡ Q 9 x
♢ K x
♣ A K Q x x

♠ A K x
♡ A 8 x x x
♢ A x x x
♣ T

ALAN (THE TORTURED DECLARER)

"Wifey led a small club and I spent the first moments staring at dummy and wondering why we weren't in hearts. We'd bid and supported them almost as many times as we had clubs. At least in hearts all I needed was to bring in the suit for a single loser, but even assuming that, I still had only eleven tricks in notrump. On this lead the only squeeze I could visualise was the one a vise was putting on my brain. Did we still think we were playing matchpoints? Then I remembered what wifey was saying when we came to the table. She always leads fourth best. That the suit had been bid only three times by the opponents was beside the point. Closing my eyes, I ducked in dummy. When I opened them my ten had won the trick! Now I led a low heart at the queen. Wifey played low smoothly, something she would never do with Kx and probably never with king third, so I stuck in the nine losing to the ten. A spade came back. I won, entered dummy with a diamond, cashed the top clubs, and put the heart queen down to complete the intra-finesse. Plus nine ninety. Thank you, Gabriel."

I laughed. "That's why we never got to play you."

"O no." Alan shook his head. "The same lady took a practice finesse in a vully game for down three, then dragged hubby kicking and screaming to a no-play slam. No one hand mattered. It was overkill, but at least it was a friendly match. I wonder which one of them is the boss in the bedroom?"

"Good partnerships transfer captaincies," Francis mused.

"Hear, hear," said Alan, and we toasted our coffee cups.

* * *

We boarded the Princess Puanani soon afterward and were immediately surrounded by four characters whose enthusiastic greetings for Francis and Alan shuffled me into the background until one of them, a gent named Jocko, introduced himself and shook my hand with the grip of a drowning man. He was crowding sixty, stood about five-four, and had a head like a billiard ball and blue eyes round as an owl's. Short wild tufts of white hair sprung in a crescent around his ears and did a Fuller brush imitation on his upper lip. A shirtless potbelly supported a pair of canary bermudas that stovepiped loosely around legs

like a flamingo. He slurred his way around an El Producto that
was jammed into the corner of his mouth.

"Wish? Wish? Had a pair of Wish Shissors once. Any
relation?"

"Yeah, but they cut me off. Glad to know you, Jocko."

"Thish here's my partner, Irv," Jocko said. "He'sh deaf in one
ear and shtubborn in the other, but the resht of hish health is
good."

"Hi Irv," I said, taking in the strange appearance of his
cadaverous features and vacant black eyes. He looked like an
extra from the cast of Night Of The Living Dead. A thick black
eyebrow underlined his forehead, not bothering to pause for a
break over the bridge of his nose. He wore his hair oil-slicked
and combed straight back, like a Mississippi riverboat gambler
bearing an uncomfortable resemblance to an anorexic Fred
Munster. Like Jocko he was attired in Hawaiian Casual. I shook
his hand.

"Hello, sonny," he said. "I'm looking forward to taking some
of your money from you." I stole a glance at Alan, whose
eyebrows shrugged at me.

"Well, Irv," I searched snappily for an ambiguity. "I like a
friendly, competitive game." Francis came to the rescue, hook-
ing a cane on his thumb and placing his hand on the shoulder
of a giant with farmboy features and hair like straw.

"This is Matthew," he said, "and over here's his partner in
crime and other things, Jeffrey. Naturally we call them Mutt and
Jeff."

"What else?" I said, shaking their hands. Jeff was even shorter
than Jocko, but slim and well-proportioned. He wore his shoe-
polish black hair strung from a part just over his left ear and
layered carefully over a scalp as slick as Jocko's and twice as
oily. His age was so indeterminate a carnival hustler couldn't
come within a decade of it. He bobbed his head to greet me and
winced a short grin. Mutt stuck out his hand.

"Howdy," he said. His voice began somewhere in his belly
and rumbled its way up a mile of oesophagus, but when he took
my hand it felt as if I were playing pattycake with a mahi-mahi.

"I guess a giant named Mutt's a bit like a midget named

Hulk," I blurted, my hoof-in-mouth timing impeccable as always.

"Like a midget named Alice," a voice like angelsilk spoke from my waistside. I turned and looked down quizzically at the smiling face of a grey-haired lady about a metre high. Granny glasses perched precariously on the end of her nose, apparently restrained from slipping completely off by a mole acting as a doorstop. She was holding a tray of sliced fruit – papaya and mango and the ubiquitous pineapple of the islands. Each piece had been stabbed with a brightly coloured plastic toothpick. I felt my cheeks flush.

"Now don't be embarrassed, young man; Michael, yes? That was really quite funny. You can call me Little Alice, like all my friends do. I've been tending things on this cruise ever since the boys started doing it."

"Thanks, Little Alice," I said, accepting some fruit.

"The rest of you boys help yourselves to this plate and get ready to come below. Breakfast in ten minutes!" She pushed the tray onto a tabletop and hobbled across the deck, throwing me a quick smile as she disappeared below. I had a new friend.

Mutt and Jeff grabbed some fruit, arguing over a bridge hand until they cornered Alan against a railing and demanded his opinion. Alan was waxing Solomonic when a bell rang and Mutt and Jeff shot for breakfast like Pavlovian dogs, leaving Alan to conclude his discourse with the ocean breeze. Jocko, who had been checking his watch and edging ever closer to the rising odour of cooked ham, nipped them at the wire. Irv ambled behind, lost in conversation with Francis.

"Who *are* these people?" I asked Alan as we lagged.

He smiled. "Friends of mine."

"That I worked out. What I can't work out is why, except for Francis and Little Alice, they all have what we used to call a Farmer's Tan. Where did you find this group? It sure as hell wasn't Hawaii."

"Well," Alan drawled, "maybe you can ask Francis after breakfast.

So I did.

*   *   *

Breakfast, laced liberally with laughter, gibes and jokes, champagne'd juices, and an occasional string of sentences that passed for conversation, was one of the more memorable meals of my life. It ended much too soon. Little Alice was hearing nothing of anybody helping her to clear up, so after coffee we all drifted topside. I found myself on the stern railing with Francis, watching the spreading wake trail behind to frame the receding island of Oahu. It was the moment I had visualised the previous day, when I had neglected to take the safety play, except that we were on the stern and not the bow.

If you need a clairvoyant, call me last.

"Alan didn't say much," Francis offered, "simply because he's too modest to say none of us would be here if not for him."

I squeezed my brow. "I don't get it. I thought *you* were throwing this party."

"Not me."

"Well, Francis, it's unusual. Alan and I have been close since school days. He tells me most things."

"He ever tell you about the old man with a ticket punched one way to hell he fished out of a mental hospital?"

"Uh...no." Boy, can I be articulate sometimes. "Uh...you?"

"Sure me." He watched my face for a reaction.

Poker-faced, that's me. "I'll be damned."

"Damned is what I was," Francis said. "I had a stroke not too long after I retired. Musta been the boredom. Left me silly a long time. Long time. Partially paralysed, couldn't talk, didn't know my own family or even my own name, for a while. By the time things started to come back I found the kids had had me put away. Set up a trust fund outta my own money to pay my bills until I croaked. The rest they took, left me to rot, recover or not. I screamed bloody murder when I realised what they'd done to me. Considering my environment it wasn't the smartest thing I've ever done. Got myself pumped with enough happy juice to last the winter. In the spring they cut down the drugs and introduced me to the lawn crowd. I knew enough to smile and say thanks. That's where I met everyone on this ship, except you and the crew. On the lawn of a New England nuthouse."

"I thought they were a little eccentric."

"Hell," Francis laughed, "even for *nuts* they're eccentric! But they're my friends, the lot of them. Trust 'em more than a dog, and the dog more than most other people I know. That's where I learned bridge, under a maple on a nuthouse lawn. The irony is that bridge is probably what kept me sane. Best pastime in the world." He looked at me. "Well, when you're my age, anyway."

"Where does Alan come in?"

"He had a great-aunt there, busy wearing out her third rocking chair. Seems nobody else paid her any attention so he dropped in on her whenever he was on the east coast. One afternoon he wandered outside and saw us playing bridge, drifted over, jawed a bit, kibitzed a while. After that he stopped to visit us whenever he came to see his aunt, and after she died he kept coming back. We all got to know each other, because we talked pretty serious with him. He never patronised us, you see, which is something others always did. Never could work out a good reason why. Alan'd give us the odd tip on our game, even sit in once in a while. But never once did he treat us any different than he would any so-called normal person in the outside world.

"Then one day he turned to me and said, 'Francis, you don't belong in here,' and two weeks later he showed up with two men, a lawyer and a psychiatrist, and within a month I was out of there. Strange feeling. Felt like I was leaving jail and leaving home at the same time.

"Alan had a two-room flat waiting for me in Boston, and everything else I needed including having the trust fund pay *me* every month instead of the hospital. Rest of it's still in the courts. Needless to say I don't send my kids Christmas cards."

"Wasn't it lonely, leaving your friends?"

"For a while, but Alan weaned me. Got me into duplicate, the dirty dog. I got to meet a lot of new people, make some new friends. Went back to visit the old gang pretty regular, 'though."

"How'd they get out, finally?"

"O, they're not out. Just their annual vacation, courtesy of Alan. He takes all the responsibility , even pays for a staff doctor to accompany them. The doctors are happier than hogs in mud with the arrangement. They draw lots every year to see who gets to come along. That's Doctor Brenner over there with the rum getting the suntan. Hardly budges from the spot. The darker the tan the bigger the hero when he returns."

"Thrilling."

"At least he stays out of the way. Last year Doc McNeil was such a pest Jocko was threatening to shove a cigar in his nether region and feed him to the sharks."

I laughed. "How long has Alan been doing this?" I asked.

"This is the fourth year. Two days of bridge and five days as tourists. They love it, and Alan too."

I shook my head and smiled, feeling very proud of my friend the Shadow. "Y'know, Francis, I know a seven-year-old kid who doesn't believe in Santa."

"Now you know one over seventy who does." Francis scratched his nose. "Why don't you grab some rays yourself, relax. We'll be playing a lot of bridge later."

"That's not a bad idea."

"If you fall asleep and start looking like a lobster I'll baste you and roll you over."

* * *

It seemed not a moment had passed while I lay timeless in the sun and the breeze when a shadow came between my closed eyelids and the warm brightness behind them.

"Shadow?" I said, sitting up suddenly.

"Francis," the silhouette standing over me said. "They're shuffling the cards. Mutt and Jeff have already started up against Irv and Jocko. You drew me."

"Great," I said as I stretched and stood. "but who's playing with Alan?"

"Why, Little Alice, of course."

"Of course."

"We're having a team match, since there's eight of us this trip. Alan showed everybody how to score while you were napping. Little Alice said she's been trying to score for years."

I laughed. "That makes them opponents. Who are our teammates?"

"Mutt and Jeff. Ten bucks an IMP. Irv says he can't wait to get at you in the second half."

"What is it that makes Irv like me so much?" I asked.

"You're a free man in Paris," Francis shrugged.

* * *

The match began.

Little Alice had served drinks all around as Alan fetched a pillow for her chair, then she perched herself atop it and proceeded to destroy Francis and me with her bidding, not that her defense left us unscathed.

Holding a shapely seven count after Alan had opened on the first hand out she managed to find three bids, two of them forcing, to land Alan in a notrump game, quietly down four. Then, holding ♠K ♡x ◇Axxxx ♣Jxxxxx, she raised a one spade opening bid by Alan to two spades! He bid game, I failed to lead a Litvack (trump), and Alan scored a heart ruff with the stiff king. Four spades, just in. A few hands later I held my first opening bid of the day:

♠AQx ♡KQx ◇x ♣T98xxx. Naturally Alan chose that moment to open one club in front of me.

"One diamond," responded Little Alice with great confidence.

"One heart," rebid Alan.

"Two diamonds," said Little Alice, not quite as confidently. It was apparent she didn't want to declare any hands she didn't have to.

"Two notrump," Alan said, perhaps reading her mind.

"Three diamonds," said Little Alice. Was that the slightest quaver of trepidation I noticed?

"Three notrump," bid Alan (anyway).

That was enough for me. Both minors not breaking, both heart honours behind his ace and the spade AQ sitting over the king he announced in the bidding.

"Double," I said, wondering if I hadn't made a slight error when Little Alice began to ponder, no doubt in the consideration of pulling to her fourth diamond. Finally she passed, and I led a top club. Little Alice apologised for having only nine points (I grinned inwardly) as she carefully laid her dummy down. I stared at: ♠xxx ♡x ◇AKQxxxxx ♣x! Alan, holding ♠Kxx ♡A9xx ◇x ♣AKQJx, remarked that I may have done a trifle better leading the ace of spades. I was just glad they weren't vulnerable.

"Not the greatest start, Francis," I said.

"There is a tiger in the lady's tank," he answered.

"Flattery won't even get you a beer in this game, boys," Little Alice retorted. "I thought about redoubling."

"Cruel, my partner's cruel," Alan muttered, suppressing a smile.

Soon after I picked up the kind of collection I usually attract at rubber bridge: ♠xx ♡Qxxx ◇JT87 ♣Kxx. After two passes Alan again got to open in front of me, this time with two spades. Little Alice raised him to three. He bid four clubs. Little Alice raised him to five. Not wanting to bid diamonds and have them raised as well Alan jumped directly to the small slam in spades. I led the diamond jack into: ♠xx ♡KJx ◇Q9x ♣Qxxxx. Alan thought about his play at trick one longer than was usual for him. Finally he played the queen, covered by Francis and won with the ace in the closed hand. Alan immediately played a heart to the jack. When that held he led a trump to the eight, again winning. A heart to the king followed and another trump to the nine. When the ace dropped Francis' king before I had a chance to play to the trick I paused to take stock. Sometimes after declarer has a suit break and two finesses work there's still a way to beat the hand.

Let's see. He started with six top spades missing the king, at least ace third in hearts, and both minor aces. That's eleven ugly tricks. If he were 6-3-1-3 he'd be playing ace and a club and claiming next; besides, why play the queen of diamonds at trick one? If he were 6-4-1-2 he would have rebid hearts; besides, I'm strip-squeezed, having to come down to three cards while holding ♠- ♡Q ◇T ♣Kx. I'd have to hold the heart queen only to get thrown in with it to lead a club; and again, why the queen of diamonds? 6-3-3-1? Naw; silly. He'd have ducked the opening lead to his ace and later hooked the nine. So he must be 6-3-2-2. A moment's more thought and I realised the hand was still cold. Now I'd ditch the heart queen only to get thrown in with the ten of diamonds. Now I knew why he'd played the queen at trick one. I was about to toss in my cards when the leprechaun of deception, who had been perched invisibly on my shoulder, gave my earlobe a hard tweak. What if I could convince Alan my seven of diamonds was a club, and my original shape had been 2-4-3-4? Perfect!

I played my middle club on the trump ace, and completed an 'echo' with my baby club on the next spade, stiffing my king. I followed to the heart ace, ditched the diamond *eight* on the penultimate trump, looking like a man who started with JT8, and on the last trump dumped the heart queen. Alan would strip the dummy down to ♠- ♡- ◇9 ♣Qx and throw me in with the diamond, when I would produce my seven for the setting trick!

Except that he tossed the club *queen* from dummy, leaving the doubleton diamond nine, and led a diamond from his hand. I was in and diddled. I put down the club king but he showed me the jack with his ace. Ho hum. Just another cactus bloom blushing unseen in the desert air.

"You must have played that very well," Little Alice smiled encouragingly to Alan as her tiny fist surrounded her pencil and entered the score.

"The play wasn't nearly as good as the defense," he said, darting a glance in my direction.

"Thanks for stopping to smell the flowers, Bra', but your play was just that much better."

"Not so. If I didn't own the jack of clubs you'd have had me. I never divined you'd stiffed the king. I would've ditched the diamond from dummy and gone down."

"If you guys are through breaking your wrists on each other's backs," Francis piped in, "I've got a bid coming."

"Sounds like an opener," said Little Alice. "How nice for a change."

"One no trump," smiled Francis.

FRANCIS
♠ K Q 8 x
♡ Q x x
♢ A Q x
♣ A T x

♠ A 9 x x x
♡ A
♢ J x x
♣ K Q 9 x
· MR.EGO

MDW	L.A.	FRANCIS	ALAN
-	-	1 NT	P
3 ♠	P	4 ♣	P
4 ♡	DBL.	P	P
5 ♣	P	5 ♢	P
5 NT	P	7 ♠	P
P	DBL.	P	P
REDBL.	P	P	P

I confess; my ego redoubled. Little Alice tabled the heart jack. Well, she had kindly told me of her JTxx of trumps, not that I would have missed the safety play. When did I ever miss safety plays? Certainly she held the heart king, and needed to have the diamond king as well if I were to make this hand. Then there was the small matter of the club jack. Why do I bid so much?

I won the heart ace and cashed the ace of spades, Alan ditching first a diamond, then a club as I led a second trump at the dummy with Little Alice splitting her honours. I ruffed a heart back to hand, finessed the eight of spades, and drew the last trump as Alan pitched one of each minor. The club ace drew a heart from Little Alice, and I could almost claim, the ending being clear. I unblocked the club ten to the queen and followed with the diamond finesse. When the queen held I played a club to the nine. This was the ending:

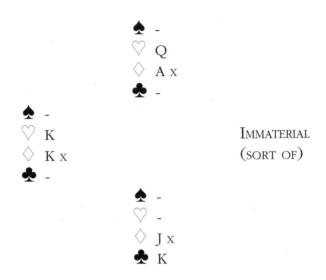

Now the club king squeezes Little Alice in the reds.

Except that Alan showed up with the heart king! Down one.

"Nice try," said Francis.

"Gosh," said Little Alice. "I should have kept my mouth shut. I thought we were finished when he got my trumps."

"We were," said Alan, "but he would have picked up your trumps anyway." I looked at him. He shrugged. "An unlucky expert hand," he said. "A dummy reversal works no matter who holds the king of hearts." I slapped my forehead.

"Don't do that, Michael. You'll hurt yourself," Little Alice said. She smiled at me and pulled her cards from the next board. I couldn't tell if she were putting me on or not.

I picked up a 1-3-3-6 yarborough as Alan opened yet another hand in front of me, this time with a game bid in spades. Little Alice squirmed, looked up hopefully at Alan, and raised him to slam. Francis glanced at Alan, smiled, and doubled.

Great, I thought, a ruff on the lead and a trick on the side. Way to go, Francis. I put a club on the track.

Now tell me the truth. If, like Francis, you held this tidy

collection: ♠A ♡AJxx ◇xxx ♣AQxxx, you might be tempted to double too, right?

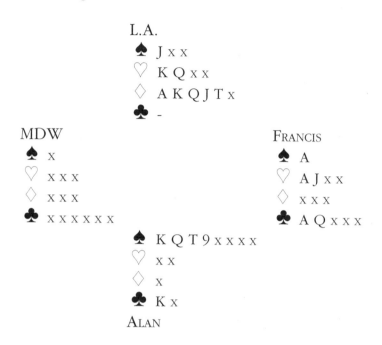

L.A.
♠ J x x
♡ K Q x x
◇ A K Q J T x
♣ -

MDW
♠ x
♡ x x x
◇ x x x
♣ x x x x x x

FRANCIS
♠ A
♡ A J x x
◇ x x x
♣ A Q x x x

♠ K Q T 9 x x x x
♡ x x
◇ x
♣ K x
ALAN

"Nice bid, Little Alice," Alan said as she tabled the dummy. Nice lead, Wiss. Alan ruffed the club and ditched his hearts on the three top diamonds. He ruffed a heart, ruffed the club king, and graciously conceded the trump ace.

"My fault," Francis said. "I knew you'd take it as Lightner, but I didn't think it would matter. So much for greed." I wrestled with my conscience, wondering if I should mention that without the double I would have led a diamond. I lost even that battle.

Then Little Alice provided living proof you don't have to be Irish to have the leprechauns on your side. With both sides vulnerable she picked up: ♠AKQT ♡QTx ◇xx ♣AQTx, and heard me open with three diamonds on her right. She doubled, and Francis' five diamond call ended the auction.

Pick a lead. I dare you.

Little Alice thought about it for a moment, then put down the spade ten! And not without confidence, I might add.

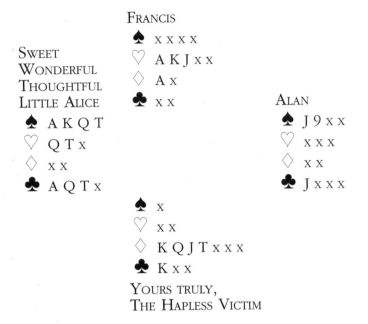

FRANCIS
♠ x x x x
♡ A K J x x
◇ A x
♣ x x

SWEET
WONDERFUL
THOUGHTFUL
LITTLE ALICE
♠ A K Q T
♡ Q T x
◇ x x
♣ A Q T x

ALAN
♠ J 9 x x
♡ x x x
◇ x x
♣ J x x x

♠ x
♡ x x
◇ K Q J T x x x
♣ K x x

YOURS TRULY,
THE HAPLESS VICTIM

Alan figured it would cost nothing to play the spade jack. When it held he looked at me and smiled, then placed his second black jack on the table. Down one. Again.

"Helluva lead," Alan and I said in unison.

"Automatic," Little Alice said humbly, parroting something she had earlier heard Alan say to Mutt and Jeff. "Since I held two suits of equal length I led fourth best from my strongest." I looked at my half-empty drink, suddenly realising it was half-full. I shrugged, threw it down in a single motion, and rose to mix myself another.

"Me, too," Alan said, joining me at the bar.

*   *   *

There was one advantage to being down forty-six IMP's at the half... Irv couldn't have much of a killer instinct.

Right. And a well-fed shark doesn't have much of a bite.

On the first board, with Irv on my right, Francis opened one diamond and I got to declare four hearts on these cards:

FRANCIS

♠ x x x
♡ A x x x
◇ A K x x
♣ A x

♠ A x x
♡ J 9 x x x
◇ Q x x
♣ K x

MOI, ABOUT TO REMAIN
THE HAPLESS VICTIM

Jocko led the spade king, and when I ducked continued with the queen. I won and led a trump to the ace. Irv dropped the king and mashed his cards into his chest, fixing me with a glare for which the adjective steely would be much too gentle. Laser is more like it. Well, now that I knew trumps weren't breaking I had to find diamonds 3-3 to pitch a spade on the good thirteener as Jocko belatedly ruffed in.

Except they were 2-4 and Jocko ruffed the third round with the ten, his only trump, cashed the spade jack, and Irv took the setting trick with the heart queen. I'd been Alcatraz Couped! *Now* Irv smiled.

Wiss' revenge, however, was not long in coming.

With both sides vulnerable I picked up in third seat: ♠Kxx ♡J ◇AKQJxxx ♣Kx. After two passes I opened three notrump and bought the hand. Had Little Alice been at the table I have no doubt the dummy delivered from Francis would have been ace and a spade, ace and length in clubs, and a doubleton diamond, and down we'd go in three notrump with a diamond slam cold. But Little Alice was wreaking her personal brand of havoc at the other table now, and when Jocko led the club jack Francis put down the dummy of my dreams:

♠xx ♡xxx ◇T9x ♣Q97xx!

The card gods are just, I mused to myself as I won in hand

and fired the suit right back. Down one wasn't going to rub Irv's nose in anything. Jocko won the ace as Irv pitched a low diamond, then went into the tank.

He scratched his nose, then an ear. He rubbed his bald pate, then his belly. The longer he stewed the more certain I was they had no off-suit carding arrangements. Finally he closed his cards and put them face down on the table. Then he reached into a pocket, pulled out a coin, and flipped it in the air. Irv's right arm shot out and snatched the coin like a frog's tongue snatching a fly.

"That's not the way we play this game, *Jerko*. I told you before. Think about it long enough and you'll find a reason to do one thing or the other."

"Give me back my quarter, *Oiving.*"

"Here. Think about it."

"I'm thinking...I've thought." And he put a small spade down, to Irv's ten and my king. Plus 630 into their slam!

JOCKO
- ♠ A 9 8 x
- ♡ Q 9 8 x
- ♢ -
- ♣ A J T 8 x

IRV
- ♠ Q J T x
- ♡ A K T x x
- ♢ x x x
- ♣ x

"Why the hell did you lead a spade away from your ace?" Irv pleaded.

"Because you told me to think about it, so I thought about it. After I took the ace of clubs I had two four card suits left, and it was notrump, so I led from my strongest one." A corollary of Little Alice's fourth best leads, no doubt. Just not quite the same measure of success.

On the very next board I picked another hand more common to what I get playing rubber bridge, and I decided to kick myself in the teeth with it.

Holding: ♠xx ♡xxx ♢xxx ♣Jxxxx I found myself on lead against seven notrump after hearing Jocko open a third seat two hearts, Irv respond spades and later blackberries, and Francis double an ensuing club call from Jocko. I decided to show Francis my entire hand on the go and tabled the jack of clubs.

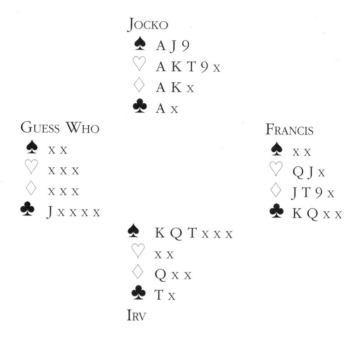

JOCKO
♠ A J 9
♡ A K T 9 x
♢ A K x
♣ A x

GUESS WHO
♠ x x
♡ x x x
♢ x x x
♣ J x x x x

FRANCIS
♠ x x
♡ Q J x
♢ J T 9 x
♣ K Q x x

♠ K Q T x x x
♡ x x
♢ Q x x
♣ T x

IRV

Well done again, Wiss. This time I'd led the setting trick in a grand, handing Irv a Vienna Coup at trick one! Not knowing what else to do, Irv won the club ace and cashed all his pointed suit winners. It was enough. He cackled as he wrote up the score.

"Well played, Oiving!" Jocko crowed along. "You ain't just another pretty face!" I grimaced. Little Alice would have beaten this hand easily - fourth best, no? The breeze through the open portholes wasn't enough to cool the perspiration on my body.

Then the pendulum swung again.

The bidding is irrelevant, mostly because neither Francis nor I wish to admit to having taken part in the auction we perpetrated. I ended up declaring four hearts on these cards:

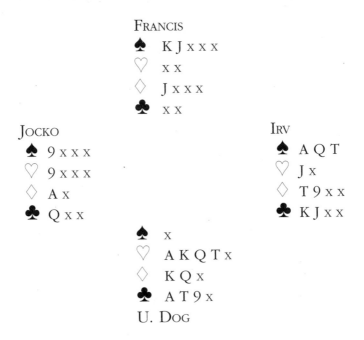

FRANCIS
♠ K J x x x
♡ x x
♢ J x x x
♣ x x

JOCKO
♠ 9 x x x
♡ 9 x x x
♢ A x
♣ Q x x

IRV
♠ A Q T
♡ J x
♢ T 9 x x
♣ K J x x

♠ x
♡ A K Q T x
♢ K Q x
♣ A T 9 x
U. DOG

Since Jocko's four card suits were identical, he decided to lead a small club, thankfully enough for me. When Irv's king held the trick he continued the suit and I was in control. I won the ace and led a spade, inserting the jack when Jocko played low smoothly. Irv won the queen and belatedly led trumps. I won the ace, ruffed a club as the queen appeared from Jocko, and led a diamond to the king and ace. Jocko led a spade, although nothing mattered anymore. I played low, ruffing Irv's ten, and led out my trumps. The jack dropped immediately from Irv, and shortly thereafter, on the penultimate trump, he felt the pressure in all three suits:

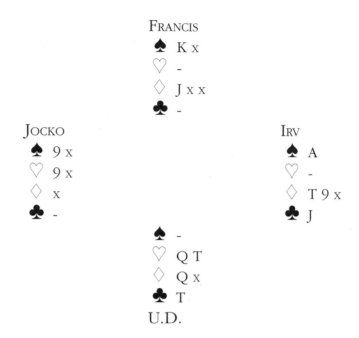

FRANCIS
♠ K x
♡ -
◇ J x x
♣ -

JOCKO
♠ 9 x
♡ 9 x
◇ x
♣ -

IRV
♠ A
♡ -
◇ T 9 x
♣ J

♠ -
♡ Q T
◇ Q x
♣ T

U.D.

I threw a spade from dummy and Irv had nowhere to go. The breeze felt cooler now.

"Lucky for you I held everything," Irv grunted.

"Luck only hurts when it's bad," I answered congenially. We'd need a lot more of it if we were to pull *this* match out of the coals. Little did I know Alan was performing some Shadow magic at the other table and our chances were even slimmer than I had estimated.

At our table, with none vulnerable, Francis started with a preempt of four clubs and we got to try out a toy we'd discussed on Saturday evening when we sat out the final session of the pairs event.

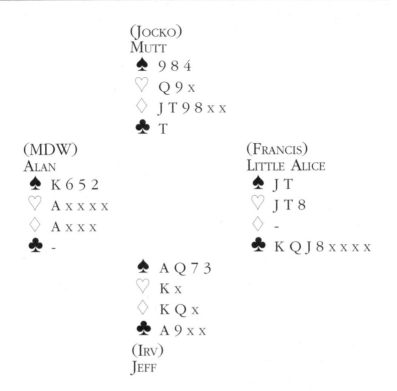

(JOCKO)
MUTT
♠ 9 8 4
♡ Q 9 x
◇ J T 9 8 x x
♣ T

(MDW)
ALAN
♠ K 6 5 2
♡ A x x x x
◇ A x x x
♣ -

(FRANCIS)
LITTLE ALICE
♠ J T
♡ J T 8
◇ -
♣ K Q J 8 x x x x

♠ A Q 7 3
♡ K x
◇ K Q x
♣ A 9 x x

(IRV)
JEFF

Irv doubled the opening call, and when Jocko bid four diamonds Francis doubled that, and I alerted the bid.

"What the hell does that mean?" Irv demanded.

"It means he doesn't have trumps, if we're playing something we discussed the other day. We agreed to play negative part-score doubles after opening a preempt. He shows either a singleton or a void in diamonds. If it's a singleton, then he shows a second singleton somewhere else. He wants to compete."

"Jeez," Irv said, "is this what duplicate does to you?"

It didn't matter what he did next; we were destined to go plus on the hand.

"I remembered," Francis beamed.

"So did I," I answered in amazement.

At the other table Little Alice was a little timid. She opened with only three clubs and Jeff bid the notrump game.

Alan led a small heart to the nine, ten, and king, and ducked diamonds until the third round. Upon taking the ace he went into a trance. When he emerged he put the *six* of spades on the table! There was no way for Jeff to extricate himself.

"The process of illumination," Alan said to me later. "Little Alice had seven or eight clubs for her bid, leaving Jeff four or five along with his known three diamonds. That left room for a maximum of six cards in the majors. If he were 3-3 there was no way to deny him his slow entry in hearts, but if he were 4-2 there was no spade holding he could have where we could not deny him dummy access, *as long as I began to unblock immediately.*"

Valiantly Jeff played low from dummy, winning the ten with the ace, then leading the queen. Alan ducked, unblocking the five, won the spade seven with the king, cashed the ♡A and threw Jeff back into his hand with the spade deuce to the three. Jeff played well from that point to give Little Alice only two club tricks, and Alan had saved his team a small bushel of IMP's.

* * *

Truisms are truisms, and time *does* fly when you're having fun. It seemed I'd hardly finished my third drink when we came to the last hand of the afternoon. Francis and I outbid Alan and Little Alice and lost thirteen IMPs for our efforts.

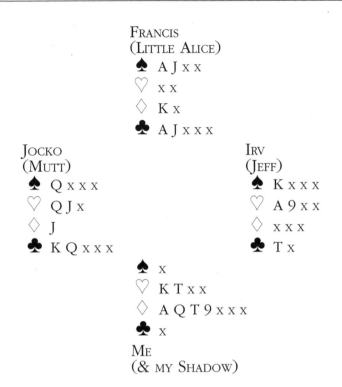

FRANCIS
(LITTLE ALICE)
♠ A J x x
♡ x x
♢ K x
♣ A J x x x

JOCKO
(MUTT)
♠ Q x x x
♡ Q J x
♢ J
♣ K Q x x x

IRV
(JEFF)
♠ K x x x
♡ A 9 x x
♢ x x x
♣ T x

♠ x
♡ K T x x
♢ A Q T 9 x x x
♣ x

ME
(& MY SHADOW)

FRANCIS	MDW	LITTLE ALICE	ALAN
1 ♣	1 ♢	1 ♣	1 ♢
1 ♠	3 ♢	1 ♠	3 ♢
3 ♡	3NT	4 ♢ (!)	4NT
P		5 ♡	6 ♢
		P	

Mutt led the club king against the slam, Alan winning and immediately leading a heart from the dummy. Jeff thought nothing was to be gained by rising with the ace and the king won in Alan's hand. He then led a low heart to Mutt's jack. Mutt switched to the card he should have led on the go, his trump jack, but now Alan won the king, ruffed a club, ruffed a heart, ruffed another club, and proceeded to run all his trumps to this three card ending:

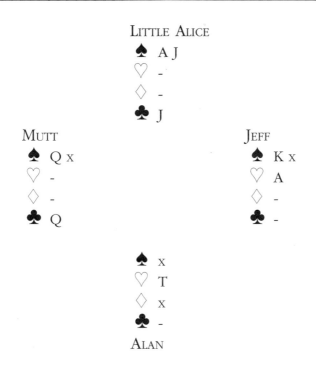

LITTLE ALICE
♠ A J
♡ -
♢ -
♣ J

MUTT
♠ Q x
♡ -
♢ -
♣ Q

JEFF
♠ K x
♡ A
♢ -
♣ -

♠ x
♡ T
♢ x
♣ -
ALAN

On the last trump Mutt had to let go a spade in order to retain the club lady. Alan ditched the now useless club jack and Jeff felt the pinch in the majors. Alan neglected to mention they had three chances to beat the hand.

"Jeffrey, why didn't you win the ace of hearts?" Mutt implored.

"Matthew, because you didn't lead a trump."

"I didn't think I had one," Mutt pouted. "I thought I had two jacks of hearts!"

* * *

I got sweet solace as we scored the half and won the battle by a single IMP. Unfortunately we'd lost the war by forty-five, which is another way of saying four hundred and fifty dollars. But who was counting?

We all went topside, where we crossgabbed the hands and watched the town of Kailua-Kona grow as we approached the harbour. Little Alice soon went below to see that the cook had dinner underway while Mutt and Jeff collared Alan and steered him to the bow to discuss the match. Jocko lit a fresh cigar and plopped himself into a deck chair, soon joined by Irv carrying drinks for both of them. Francis hooked his canes over his forearms and leaned his bony wrists on the rail beside me. Already we could hear the surf on the shoreline.

"Enjoy yourself?" he asked.

"Sure, are you kidding?! It was great. I'm not too ecstatic about losing four hundred and fifty bucks, but I had a helluva lot of fun doing it. By the way, who gets my money? Tell me it's not Irv. Little Alice can have every cent I've got but every dime to Irv is a drop of my blood."

Francis chuckled. "You don't pay anyone. Alan covers everybody's action and Little Alice keeps the books. Loser's funds go into the kitty for next year's trip."

"Why didn't you clue me in?"

"Wanted to see how you handled watching your money dwindle."

"How'd I handle it?"

"Like you never had it in the first place. Listen, what do you say we play a set game? I know some fellows in Honolulu who're a little ripe and about ready to pluck."

I laughed. "I like your altitude, Francis. Sure, why not? I plan on being on the islands for a while."

"Plan on staying at my place?" a voice said behind me. Silent as a shadow Alan had appeared from nowhere. I clutched my chest.

"Why do you keep doing that to me? ...Sure, I'll be around. First another week in Lahaina, then I'll come by." I turned back to Francis. "You and I can get that game in after that. I'll call you from Alan's and we can make arrangements."

"You're on. I'm going below for a little nap before dinner. We eat right after we dock." His canes tick-tocked the deck as he ambled away.

"Quite the old gentleman," I said as Francis disappeared below, "and quite the group of characters you've adopted."

"Francis filled you in?"

"Yup."

"I plead guilty."

We stood in silence for long moments, watching the town take on a glow in the amber rays of the setting sun.

"There going to be more bridge after dinner?"

"Not for you and me. We're going out on the town. Francis always retires early, and the rest will play rubber until they fall asleep at the table."

*   *   *

Shortly afterward we docked and immediately Little Alice rang the dinner bell. Once again I had trouble picking my way through the laughter to get at the food. It seemed only moments before dinner was over, coffee and dessert were downed, and the cards were being cut for rubber.

Alan and I begged off and Francis came topside with us to say goodnight. In the dark evening Kailua was brightly lit and alive with the bustle of tourists. Overhead the sky seemed to pulse with the brightness of the myriad stars, alive as the clear night sky of Saskatchewan. The salt breeze, tinged with the sweetness of a recent shower, wafted the hair I used to have.

"It's been a wonderful time," Francis said to us. "Thanks both of you, for everything. I'll see you in the morning."

"What are you thanking me for?" I asked. "I'm the one that's grateful."

"You?" Francis said as Alan and I stepped onto the dock. "I got my gold card playing with you on Saturday. Why did you think I took the night off?" He grinned a goodnight and tick-tocked his way below.

The Shadow and I headed for Angie's to begin the evening with a beer and a few games of pool.

Shadow Under the Palms

THE SHADOW AND I HUNG AROUND the Big Island for a few days, catching up on old times, creating a few new ones. Then he left for Honolulu to meet Francis and the funny folk, who had continued on their cruise. I remained on the Big Island in a vain attempt to locate a transcendently attractive redhead acquaintance from Saskatoon who had moved to Hawaii to run marathons. I guess we all have our reasons.

After a few days of fruitless searching from Kailua to Captain Cook and a few nights hanging around Angie's shooting pool with the locals and trying to get lucky I got bored and hopped a plane to Maui.

The flight from Kailua-Kona to Kahului on Maui is a short one, unless your seat companion happens to be afflicted with motormouth, or perhaps B.O. induced by fear of flight. This time I had to endure both. To make matters worse, my companion was a young woman, the kind who turns heads at beaches, certainly the kind I would have been happy to meet any of the three previous evenings. I didn't know whether to charm her or change seats. Ensconcing my face in a copy of The Bridge World didn't work.

The moment the plane left the ground she grasped my upper arm with both sweaty hands and pulled herself closer to me. When we leveled off she released my arm, remained close, and began to chat my ear canal raw. Unconsciously I found myself leaning backward, trying to space myself from the ripeness, as it were, but this brought my knee into unfortunate contact with hers. She returned the pressure.

Among better bridge players thinking fast is a common attribute, thinking *too* fast a common failing. I like to think according to the occasion... one step faster than the opposition is a good rule of thumb.

I offered my current opposition a drink, which on a flight of this nature does not include the brandy I was hoping to rest under my nose. It does, however, include guava juice, my least favourite nectar of the islands insofar as it has the ironic odour of armpit and the viscosity of phlegm. But with my nose buried in the glass I was able to lean forward in a more appropriate social listening pose, while at the same time extricating my knee in an attempt to avoid the encouragement of any further scenarios.

"I see you play bridge," she said, indicating the magazine on my lap.

"Uh...yeah," I stammered, a bit surprised the tack of her talk had steered away from herself and the obvious fact that getting a pilot's license was not high on her list of Hobbies To Take Up. "Don't tell me you do..."

"No, not me...well, a little. Just a bit at home with my parents. But a friend of mine in Wailuku plays. He's really quite good. Maybe you know him? His name's Yawn."

"Wait a minute. Yawn Dyck?"

"You *do* know him!"

"I'm on my way to rent a jeep from him right now! But I didn't know he played bridge." Yawn was an old acquaintance with whom I used to share soyburgers and pakalolo at a roadside tavern in Paia. In all the hours we spent elbowhunkering discussing women, pakalolo, and the easy island life, somehow the topic of bridge had never come up. What a curious way to find out, I thought. In Hawaii, magic is afoot.

"Sometimes he plays a lot. Once he even stood me up so he could play."

"No kidding," I said, perhaps a bit too charmingly for my own good, "some guys sure have a weird sense of priorities."

"Don't they, 'though?" she said demurely over her glass. Her knee had resumed contact, and remained glued to mine until we were on the ground.

Fortunately Dyanne (she insisted I learn the spelling) was met at the airport by her mother and was heading in the opposite direction, Upcountry near Pukalani. I had neither to offer nor accept a ride. I cabbed it the few miles from the airport in Kahului to Yawn's workshop in Wailuku, where I found him tinkering on an old Mustang in the yard. After amenities I told him about meeting Dyanne on the flight over, and learning that he played bridge.

"Sure," Yawn said, running a hand through his short, sun-bleached hair. "I learned back when I was at S.F.U. You play, too? How come you never mentioned it before?"

"Usually the last thing on my mind when I'm visiting paradise."

"I suppose. But when you've lived here a few years it's a good antidote for island fever."

"How come *you* never mentioned it before?"

"When we were sharin' boo, Bra', I didn't *have* island fever. Now a day hardly goes by I don't think about movin' back to the Bay area." He shook his head ruefully. I took pity.

"Maybe it's just homesickness and not island fever. A good visit back might be all the cure you need."

"Can't afford the time away right now. Maybe after the tourist season."

"Then maybe some bridge to pack away the woes for awhile. There a club near here?"

"No clubs. There's a game in Kihei once or twice a week, I think, but I don't like duplicate much. I've played in a few tournaments and people are just too damn uptight. I play rubber bridge, that's about it."

"You mean, for money?" I enquired innocently.

"Hell, yes. Dime a point. That's ten bucks a hundred."

"Yeah, that's a lot."

"And you won't see anyone in our games get nasty, Bra'. No matter how much they lose. I mean, what makes masterpoints more important than money?"

"They're not. But pride is, and that's what most players put on the line in tournaments. To some, at least in the heat of the moment, it's more important than their behaviour."

"Perhaps..."

"Trust me. Even my behaviour may have succumbed to it, once or twice."

"You oughta play with us sometime. It'd be a nice change. My buddy Lenny and me usually play set with some guys up in Kaanapali, but nobody'd mind playing Chicago if you want to sit in. Could use a little new blood."

I resisted an urge to lick my lips. "Well, I'm on my way Upcountry to visit a friend. That's why I need the jeep. But he's a player," I said truthfully, just not saying he was a *player*. "Maybe we can both come into town for a day..."

He jumped on it. "Sure. Even better. We can swing three set pairs. How about tomorrow?"

I was beginning to wonder who was hustling whom. "How about the day after tomorrow? Maybe. I don't know my friend's plans."

"Sure. If you're here by noon we'll play, if not, then the next day. Everything's loose in the islands, Bra'."

"You got a nice jeep for me?"

"Only one. Hole in the muffler I haven't fixed. Just appeared the other day. You get a discount 'cause we're buds and another for the hole. But we have to do the paperwork."

"Deal."

As he tossed me the keys he said, "I know where Dyanne lives in Pukalani, if you're interested. She's a lotta fun."

"Thanks, Yawn, but if I were interested I'd al*ready* know where to find her." I hopped into the jeep.

"Yeah, well hang loose, Bra'." He wiggled the traditional closed fist with extended thumb and pinky at me and disappeared into his shop.

*   *   *

I decided to take the long and low road to Kula with a detour through Wailea to Little Makena Beach, with not only the best bodysurfing on Maui, but the last vestige of the terminally topless (and occasionally bottomless) as well. It was impossible to resist the Pacific's invitation of a short dip before jamming the jeep into four-wheel drive and grinding up the western slope of Haleakala into Kula by the back door, where Alan's cottage nestled far enough from the beaten track to discourage all but the most determined visitor.

The lush flora thickened as the air thinned and the road up the mountainside narrowed. Within twenty minutes I had gone from desert to garden country. I stopped a couple of times on the occasional plateau to view the exquisite vista of the Maui sunside that had spread out below me, sweeping down the mountain to the beaches, then out to sea with light-streaked water all the way to Kahoolawe and Lanai, punctuated only by the tiny isle of Molokini. Here and there sideroads turned into the bush, entrances guarded by gates, or no trespassing signs, or in one instance a rusted and overturned vehicle riddled with bullet holes. The mountain leveled off near Kula country as cattle-dotted fields appeared, edged with farmhouses or small settlements.

After two false turns and a final thrust through a hundred metres of trail overgrown with bush, I emerged into the Shadow's front yard. Fifty more metres up the hill I could see him sitting on his front porch, feet propped on the railing, two tall glasses beside the feet, and an unmistakable grin plastered on his face.

"Wiss, you jerk!" he greeted me traditionally, not having to raise his voice in the complete silence that suddenly enveloped us as I turned off the jeep's engine. "I could hear you coming halfway up the mountain!"

"Sorry," I grinned, waving as I trudged up the hill. "A new muffler didn't come with the price."

"Thought you could use a tall one," Alan said as I hauled myself onto the porch, puffing a bit.(The incline and the altitude; age and smoking don't have a damn thing to do with it!) He handed me one of the glasses. "Papaya juice and soda, swirl of Galliano. Great stuff with lots of ice."

"Just no guava," I pleaded. I settled in beside him and we caught up on the week. All had gone well in Honolulu. Francis was settling in comfortably in his new condo and the funny folk had flown home to New England, a sunblistered Doctor Brenner in tow. Alan showed me around, pointing out the new pear(avocado) trees he'd planted since my last visit, the deep whirlpool tub and shower bordered with rocks and camouflaged in the backyard greenery of hibiscus and palm and plumeria, the new sundeck over his studio/library.

"A home away from home," I said, not without envy.

"You can call it home whenever you like, you know that," Alan said. "All it really lacks is ladies...to make up a foursome for bridge, of course."

"Naturally. Speaking of that, bridge I mean, maybe you'd be into some set rubber after I unwind for a day or two. I ran into someone in Wailuku who likes to lose in pleasant dime games."

"I drool at the very thought," he laughed, "but what do you need to unwind from?"

"Four nights in a row at Angie's. Got to be a bit much."

"I have just the thing...a pakalolo appetiser followed by barbecued mahi-mahi, and island dessert."

"Double appetiser, please. Let's hold dinner for a while."

* * *

Three days later we pulled into Wailuku and found Yawn tinkering with the same Mustang. Always best to keep them waiting, I thought.

"Yawn," I called, "Meet Charley." The Shadow had donned a walrus moustache and sunglasses for the occasion. "You ready for that rubber game?"

"Hi, yeah, but we were hoping you'd make it yesterday." He wiped his hands on a rag and shook hands with Alan. "My partner can't make it today, but you guys can play set. I don't mind a kibitz anyway."

"You sure?" Alan asked. "We could play Chicago."

"Nah, it'd just mess up the game. I'd like to watch. Maybe you guys'll be luckier than we've been lately. Yesterday cost us eighty ways. Eight hundred bucks. Does me in for the week and then some."

"Pretty good, are they?" Alan said.

"Not bad, but sometimes they seem to hold cards like they're playing pinochle. And their leads are dynamite."

Alan and I exchanged a glance. This had all the earmarks of a wire. Alan shrugged.

"Okay," I said, "where do we play?"

"Johnson's place. Kaanapali. I'll give him a call and say we're on the way." Yawn disappeared inside the shop. I turned to Alan.

"What do you think?"

"I think I want to stop at a drugstore on the way, pick a few things up, just in case."

"What do you mean 'just in case'?"

"In case we're in a place we want to get out of quick."

A few minutes later Yawn hopped into the back of the jeep and we were off, heading south to Maalea before turning west toward Lahaina and Kaanapali. Alan twisted around in his seat.

"Tell me about Johnson and his partner, Yawn." Alan asked.

"Not much to tell. Johnson's a fat cat; likes to play under the palms in his backyard whenever the wind is down. Bids a lot, doesn't play them too well. Nobody knows his partner's name, but everybody calls him Shooter. I think he got the handle in Vegas, at the crap tables. He's a bit of a sleaze, a much better cardplayer than Johnson, and a pretty good bidder. But they're both something else on opening leads, or even the suit to switch to in the middle of the hand. That's about all I know, except that they don't often lose, and when they do it isn't by much."

"Think we're getting in over our heads, Charley?" I asked Alan.

"We'll be all right," he said. "If anything funny starts going down, just remember to follow my lead."

"You think these guys are cheating or something?" Yawn piped in. "I wouldn't put it past Shooter, for sure."

"Let's just say it sounds like they're defying the odds a bit," Alan said. "You know them better than we do."

"Well, I'm with you whatever happens. I'll just be a good kibitzer and keep in the background."

*　*　*

An hour later we were under the palms in Fat Cat's back yard.

Yawn had named him aptly. Both his body and his .environment testified that he liked to spend money, mostly on himself. Shooter on the other hand was slim enough to stand sideways behind a palm and disappear. He dressed yuppie Hollywood, down to the rings and bracelet and gold neckwear. I guessed he even wore Gucci gotchees.

Fat Cat was amiable and talkative. He served drinks after getting everybody comfortable and won himself the cut for deal, keeping up a bright banter as he slid the cards across the table.

"Rather play day than night," he said, "and rather out than in. Much sharper early, and the fresh air's good if you've had a Mai-Tai or two with lunch. Long as the damn wind isn't blowing too hard, that is. I oughta invest in those magnetic cards one of these days. Play in a damn hurricane then."

The first two hands were quiet, each side bidding and making one notrump. Then Alan picked up:

♠AKxx ♡ATx ♢9xx ♣AT9 and heard Shooter start with three hearts on his left, which was passed around to him. Game in notrump seemed automatic, but Shooter suddenly shot out four hearts, back once again to Alan. He decided to find out where these guys were at and put his bread (and mine) in the blender and trotted out a four spade call, passed around to Fat Cat whose resounding double fluttered the fronds overhead. Alan prudently retreated back to notrumps and Shooter doubled in order to save Fat Cat any further wear and tear on his vocal chords.

It's so much fun being helpless in these situations, I thought, tabling my dummy after Shooter led the heart king.

ME

♠ J x
♡ x x
◇ K J 8 x x
♣ K 8 x x

♠ A K x x
♡ A T x
◇ 9 x x
♣ A T 9
& MY SHADOW

Alan was mildly surprised to see Fat Cat follow to the lead,
which he ducked while considering how to play the diamond
suit. It was apparent that if Shooter held the ace our lights would
shortly be shot out, so he guarded against the ten winning a later
round and floated the nine. Fat Cat gobbled up the trick with the
ten and switched to a spade, the king fetching the lady from the
Shooter. Things were looking up. Another diamond brought the
third lady from Shooter's hand, Fat Cat topping the king and
continuing spades, won with the jack. The jack of diamonds left
this ending, Fat Cat and Shooter having book in the bag:

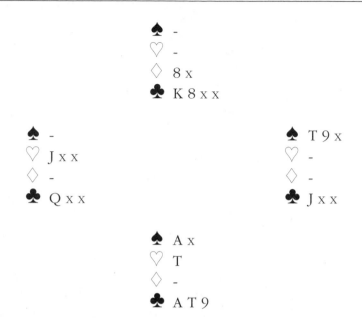

♠ -
♡ -
◇ 8 x
♣ K 8 x x

♠ -
♡ J x x
◇ -
♣ Q x x

♠ T 9 x
♡ -
◇ -
♣ J x x

♠ A x
♡ T
◇ -
♣ A T 9

On the diamond eight Fat Cat could afford a spade and Shooter a heart, but on the final diamond Fat Cat felt the pressure and was forced to ditch a club. Alan threw his now useless baby spade as Shooter bared the heart jack, then played a club to the ace. The spade ace put the final screws to Shooter, who was also forced to ditch a club, and the club eight became Alan's tenth trick. The double squeeze was all the more enjoyable by watching Alan feign innocence as Fat Cat and Shooter squirmed in turn.

"I was sure I had a trick coming," Fat Cat said.

"You did in four spades," Shooter retorted. "Why the hell can't you leave well enough alone?"

"Sorry about that," Alan apologised. "It was a bit of a flyer."

"Cards were lying awful lucky for you, Bra'," Yawn piped in.

"I still want to know where my trick went," Fat Cat said.

"You do attract the ladies," I said to Shooter. "You held all four of them." Shooter lifted his eyebrows and glanced at me over his shades with eyes as dark as a deer dropping. I could see flattering chitchat would get me about as far as the nearest reef.

On the following hand I dealt myself another of my more common collections at rubber bridge:

♠QJ ♡Txxx ◇xx ♣Txxxx. (Playing in a pairs game in San

Francisco a few weeks earlier I held a twenty-eight *and* a thirty-one pointer in the same session!) This time Fat Cat and Shooter showed they too knew how to overbid.

SHOOTER	FAT CAT
♠ K 9 8 x x	♠ A T x x
♡ K x x x	♡ A
♢ -	♢ A Q x x x
♣ K Q J x	♣ x x x

—	1 ♢
1 ♠	4 ♠
6 ♠	P (DBL)
REDBL.	P

As soon as I heard Shooter bid the slam I had my mental thumb on the jack of spades. Alan's double told me he had something nice over Fat Cat's diamonds, or no clubs, and as I briefly wondered which Shooter's redouble left me no doubt the diamonds were irrelevant. I led a club.

Alan won the ace and switched to a heart. On the ace of spades I played the jack and Shooter led another to the nine.

"Damn," he muttered as I scored my queen. "Three indications to take the finesse..."

"What three?" said Fat Cat. "With nine you play for the drop."

"Restricted choice," Yawn piped in, a kibitzer's code of silence extending only from the first bid to the last play, after all. Between hands nothing was sacrosanct.

"What the hell's that?" said Fat Cat, still miffed because *he* would have made the hand.

"Also," Shooter went on, ignoring Fat Cat's bleating, "the bidding. I figured Charley needed more than just diamonds behind dummy besides his ace. He needed trumps."

"Sorry, pard," Alan said to me, "bad double." He scored up our plus.

"Then," Shooter persisted, "there's the Law of Symmetry. A

singleton honour in dummy suggested another somewhere else in the hand."

"You were right," Alan said, "but they were both stiff aces."

· · ·

The next hour brought the flattest succession of hands I have ever seen. Half a dozen were thrown in and the remainder were low-level partscores, most played our way and most nipped a trick or two when Fat Cat and Shooter lived up to Yawn's observation of their opening leads and interior defense. They finally scored a game by adding up three one notrump contracts. Yawn dozed in his chair.

Then the flatness came to an abrupt and extreme halt when I was dealt a gang sploid. What's that, you ask? Well, since a gang splinter is a hand with two singletons...

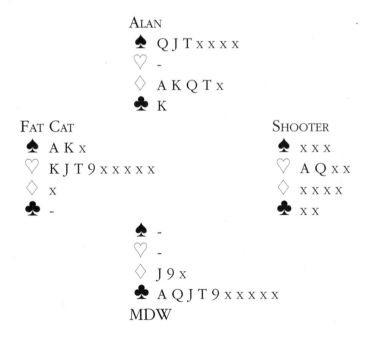

ALAN

♠ Q J T x x x x
♡ -
♢ A K Q T x
♣ K

FAT CAT

♠ A K x
♡ K J T 9 x x x x x
♢ x
♣ -

SHOOTER

♠ x x x
♡ A Q x x
♢ x x x x
♣ x x

♠ -
♡ -
♢ J 9 x
♣ A Q J T 9 x x x x x

MDW

I started proceedings with game in clubs, overcalled in hearts by Fat Cat. Alan raised me to slam and Shooter thought he had enough to support his partner as well. Had either of my majors contained a spot card I would have passed, but I decided this hand was an exception and bid one more for the road.

Poor Fat Cat. He stewed long enough to light a fresh cigar and suck down half an inch of it. He knew he was going minus if he bid seven hearts, so in a disgruntled tone he doubled and smacked down the spade king.

Well, some minuses are better than others. Fat Cat bit off the end of his cigar.

"So much for the flat hands," Yawn yawned. "I was beginning to fall asleep."

"I need a break," Alan said, his eyes motioning me toward the house. "Where's the can?"

"And I could use some cold water," I said quickly. "Where's the kitchen?"

"Kitchen's right inside the back door," Fat Cat said. "Can's down the hall on your left."

Alan and I headed for the house. As soon as we were out of earshot he muttered under his moustache, "We'd better beg out of here as soon as we can; these guys are definitely wired. We've been lucky most of the hands have been flat. Could you believe some of those leads?"

"Whaddaya mean? I mean how?"

"Fat Cat's cigar for sure; and Shooter's no chain smoker. He hardly inhales. They've been signalling by how they hold them in their mouths. Right side a diamond, centre a heart, left a spade, and clubs in the ashtray."

"Jeez," I breathed, "how did you sniff them out?"

"The first time I bid a non-suit and Shooter led it from a broken holding. It didn't take long to figure out how."

"Now what?"

"No doubt by the time we get back they'll have switched the order one way or another, so pay attention the first few hands they defend."

"But how do we get out of here without them getting wise? That Shooter looks mean."

"You aren't just being paranoid. That bulge under his armpit isn't a benign tumour. Don't worry about it. Bring me some water too, and whatever happens, follow my lead."

I was waiting at the table when Alan returned. "Here," I said, handing him a glass of water, "thought you might want one too."

"Thanks." Alan sat down, squinted, wiped his forehead with the palm of his hand. The afternoon sun had slid under the fronds of a tall palm, bathing him in light. "Mind if we move the table? Sun's too hot here...getting a bit dizzy..."

Fat Cat was quick to oblige. "No, no. Not atall," he said immediately, struggling to his feet and indicating to Shooter to take one side of the table. "Want you to be as comfortable as possible," he oozed. You had to be there to believe how sweet the syrup was that he was pouring.

As Yawn stood to move his chair and Shooter and Fat Cat were distracted with the table Alan winked and flashed me a toothy grin, revealing a large white tablet clamped between his teeth. In a moment his tongue had snatched it from sight and tucked it into the pocket of his cheek, where like a holstered sidearm it lay waiting. We settled back into the shade and resumed the game.

The card gods, on certain days, can be really friendly sorts. Probably this is to balance out the days when suits break bad, key cards are always in the wrong hand, distributions are diabolically mirrored, and partners revoke.

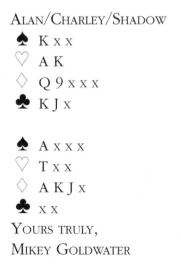

ALAN/CHARLEY/SHADOW
♠ K x x
♡ A K
◇ Q 9 x x x
♣ K J x

♠ A x x x
♡ T x x
◇ A K J x
♣ x x
YOURS TRULY,
MIKEY GOLDWATER

Alan opened one notrump, and after a forcing Stayman auction we landed in the diamond slam from my side. Clever.

Fat Cat's cigar puffed merrily from the right corner of his mouth. Shooter led a club out of turn.

After we straightened out the auction in their minds I had to decide on my options. At the time declaring myself dummy wasn't one of them. Since then, of course, the rules have been changed to protect players (such as myself) from the misapplication of Goldwater's Rule, namely that if an opponent doesn't know *whose* lead it is, they sure as hell don't know *what* to lead. Then I recalled what Alan had said about the cigar in the right corner. It was a diamond flag, which meant that they had to have changed signals as he had indicated they might. By moving them one over right became clubs, centre diamonds, left hearts, and spades in the tray. We'd bid every suit but clubs up to the five level and Alan had gone on to six; he had to have a club control, and Fat Cat had been flagging clubs. I told Shooter to put his card back in his hand.

"Lead a club," I said to Fat Cat. Clever. The deuce hit the table.

Now what would Fat Cat do, having been told to lead the suit against a slam? Wouldn't he cash the ace if he had it? But then why would he flag clubs holding only the queen? No, he has the ace or both ace and queen. Either way the king had to be right. I flew and it held.

FAT CAT	SHOOTER
♠ J x	♠ Q T 9 x
♡ x x x x	♡ Q J 9 x
♢ T x x	♢ x
♣ A x x x	♣ Q T 9 x

Three rounds of trumps and another club left Shooter on lead to come a slightly tardy spade. I won the king, ruffed dummy's last club, cashed the heart ace king, and the baby trump. The Curse of Scotland squeezed Shooter in the majors. He kept shaking his head throughout the hand.

"My fault," he said. "My fault."

"I was going to lead a spade, since you didn't know what to

lead," Fat Cat said idiotically. Blurting along, he asked, "Would
that have helped?"

Alan was already dealing the next hand. He paused in the
middle to take a deep breath and swab his forehead once again.

"You okay?" I asked.

"Sure, fine," he said, resuming the deal.

"We're just starting. Long afternoon ahead," said Fat Cat.
"You're not going to poop out, are you? I guess we could move
inside if it's too hot for you."

"No," Alan insisted, "really. I'm okay; let's play."

And once again I picked up a not untypical hand when
money was on the line:

♠x ♡x ♢98xxxx ♣JTxxx. Since the vulnerability was unfavourable there could be no thought of unusual action if Alan
passed, not that I had to worry, since he started out with two
notrump. I tried three diamonds and Fat Cat was right in there
with three spades. Alan apparently didn't think we were going
to get rich from the penalty and bid three notrump, which I was
having none of, running to four clubs. Fat Cat found another of
his frond-flapping doubles, which sent Alan into thought.
Finally he bid game in diamonds.

"Double," said Shooter, reaching for a cigarette.

"Do you mind not smoking for a bit?" Alan asked as his left
hand reached the cigarette a moment before Shooter's. "I think
that's what's been bothering me." With a smile at Shooter he
nonchalantly stubbed out the butt. "Your lead," he said to Fat
Cat.

Fat Cat stalled, appearing to go into deep thought.

"You don't mind if I chew on a dry one, do you?" Shooter
smiled, pulling out another smoke. "Makes me nervous unless
I'm chewing on something..." His glance assured me he'd rather
be gnawing on Alan's throat.

"Have some gum," I offered, quickly shoving a pack of
Trident at Shooter. Swift. Sometimes I'm very swift.

"No thanks," he said. "I don't like sugarless." He jammed the
unlit smoke into the right corner of his mouth.

If they gave an Oscar for overacting Fat Cat would have won
it in unanimity for his ensuing performance. He squirmed, he

twisted, he agonised, never looking up. He pulled out first one card and then another, finally pinching his pudgy digits on the club ace. Even after bringing it within an inch of the felt he snatched it back, played eenie-meenie with it, then thumbed it down with an air of decisiveness.

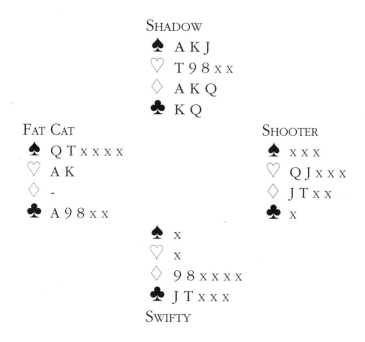

SHADOW
♠ A K J
♡ T 9 8 x x
♢ A K Q
♣ K Q

FAT CAT
♠ Q T x x x x
♡ A K
♢ -
♣ A 9 8 x x

SHOOTER
♠ x x x
♡ Q J x x x
♢ J T x x
♣ x

♠ x
♡ x
♢ 9 8 x x x x
♣ J T x x x
SWIFTY

Fat Cat stared at Shooter's spot for half a minute, keeping up the act, then continued the suit. Shooter ruffed, returning a heart to the cigar clenched tightly in the left corner of Fat Cat's mouth, and a further club promoted a second undertrick. There was no danger of Fat Cat trying to cash a second heart...Shooter's smoke still hadn't budged. Now *there* was partnership trust.

Five hundred in the glue when a heart lead saves us thirty dollars and a spade hands us game and rubber. Alan reached for his glass and swallowed half the contents in a single gulp.

"Nice defense," I said to Fat Cat with not a trace of sarcasm. Now *that* was no slight performance.

"Thanks," he nodded with smug satisfaction. "Club lead didn't work out so well last time so I thought I'd give it another shot."

Yeah, as if the situation were identical. Out of the corner of
my eye I could see Yawn shaking his head.

"Maybe you'll get another chance," he said. "Best of three."
Prophetic words. Sort of.

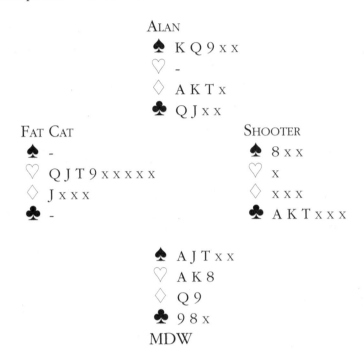

ALAN
♠ K Q 9 x x
♡ -
♢ A K T x
♣ Q J x x

FAT CAT
♠ -
♡ Q J T 9 x x x x x
♢ J x x
♣ -

SHOOTER
♠ 8 x x
♡ x
♢ x x x
♣ A K T x x x

♠ A J T x x
♡ A K 8
♢ Q 9
♣ 9 8 x
MDW

Shooter passed, I opened one spade, and Fat Cat lost no time
in bidding game in hearts, giving Alan a problem. He wiped his
forehead once more, appearing a bit redfaced. A cuebid of either
red suit would solve nothing, as there was no way for Alan to
determine whether or not I held a club control. Huffing and puffing
a bit, he simply punted it and hoped for the best. Shooter doubled,
his cigarette still hanging dry in the right corner of his mouth.

And once again Fat Cat went into his act, the histrionics
muted this time by some genuine puzzlement, insofar as he
didn't have what he knew he wanted to lead.

I glanced at Alan, whose face by this time was almost beet-
red, the colour spreading swiftly down his neck and arms. He
looked as if he were having a heart attack.

Then he winked at me.

Fat Cat glanced up at Shooter, who was glaring across the table. In frustration he slapped down the queen of hearts, Alan tabling the dummy as Shooter growled under his breath. I ruffed safely with the nine, drew trumps, and cashed the heart ace king, throwing clubs from dummy. Since Fat Cat hadn't led a club, he simply hadn't any, so he was exactly 0-9-4-0. I cashed the queen of diamonds and led the nine to the ten, hoping the odds were just.

"Another gang sploid," I said, looking up. Alan was slumping in his chair.

"Hey, Charley doesn't look so hot," Yawn said. Everybody had by now taken notice. Alan was now the hue of a boiled lobster. He was breathing in short gasps and slowly rolling his eyes.

"Jesus Aitch, he's having a stroke!" Fat Cat's cigar fell to the lawn as he jumped to his feet.

"My pills..." Alan hoarsely croaked, trying to reach into his pocket. I was at his side in a moment, reaching, digging, extracting a small bottle. "One...under my tongue!" he choked at me. Where are the talent scouts when you need them? I popped one of the tiny tablets into his mouth. He immediately screwed up his face as if he were sucking on a lemon.

"Call an ambulance!" Fat Cat yelled at Shooter.

"No," Alan breathed, "I'll be all right. Just lemme rest for a minute...It's angina...I'll be okay."

"I ain't so sure," said Shooter. Good, I thought, he's hooked. It was hard to tell behind those shades.

"He looks like he belongs in a hospital," Yawn said. Ah, uncoached amateur talent, just when you need it.

"The nearest hospital's in Wailuku," Fat Cat said. "That's almost an hour. There's a clinic in Lahaina."

"Clinic might not be a bad idea," Alan said, looking at me for confirmation.

"That's just fifteen minutes," I said, helping Alan to his feet. "You okay to walk?"

"Yeah, fine." We started toward the jeep, going only a few steps when he whispered, "Get the winnings, dummy..."

"Yawn, I can handle him," I said over my shoulder. "You mind collecting for us? Thanks for the game, guys. Maybe we can have another go at it next week..."

I poured Alan into the jeep and kept up the pretense by helping him to strap in in case Fat Cat and Shooter still had an eye on us from the house. Yawn joined us a minute later, hopping in as I gunned the engine and sprayed gravel as we shot away. As soon as we rounded the first corner Alan began laughing. He turned to Yawn, his hand out.

"What's the number?"

Yawn handed him a small wad of bills. "Sixty-five ways. Six hundred and fifty each. Thirteen hundred bucks. Are you okay?" He cocked his head quizzically at Alan.

"Strong as Stradivarius. The red'll be gone in a few minutes. It's good for you, actually. Brings the blood right to the end of the capillaries, improves the circulation."

"All right," I laughed along. "What the hell *was* that stuff?"

"Niacinamide. Vitamin bee-twelve, a gram of it. There's no after effects, except you feel better."

"Where'd you learn that?"

"A slightly schizoid buddy of mine...uses it for medication. Really does the trick. I used it once before to get out of a poker game I shouldn't have been in."

"Then what was that little pill I gave you? The sour one."

"Sour, my ass. It was saccharine! You ever eaten one of those straight?"

* * *

Fifteen minutes later we were in Lahaina, parked outside the Sunrise, heading in for an afternoon cappuccino.

Alan clued Yawn into Fat Cat and Shooter's wire, and he was so grateful he forgave the rental on the jeep.

"I couldn't say for sure if Shooter's a mechanic," Alan added. "If he is either he didn't try it, or he's too damn good for me to notice it. I suspect the former; we all held a fair share of the cards."

"You aren't really planning on going back next week, are you, Bra'?" Yawn said to me.

I looked at him. "What do you think?"

"Not without an armed escort," he drawled.

Shadow Over America

JACK KENNEDY MAY HAVE COME THE closest of any politician to have wrested a vote from me, but the airport that bore his name has never been a favourite of mine. Perhaps it's because the intelligence of large crowds, unlike the sharpness of its elbows, is inversely proportionate to its size. Individuals can be stupid enough; groups, and most especially committees, can sometimes scrape up the smarts of the average troglodyte; mobs, on the other hand, are by their nature mindless, and swayed easier than a sapling in a summer storm.

I was executing a pet manoeuvre I call the Weave and Sidle in a vain attempt to pass unbruised through a gauntlet of suitcases and elbows. All this for the dubious privilege of queuing up for a flight vacancy that was unlikely to appear. I was carrying my suitcase edgewise before me, sidestepping and dodging and excusing myself, when a hand reached from the crowd and slapped down on my shoulder. Over the commando calls of household pantwearers, the whipped whines of their mates, the hapless squalls of their offspring, a penetrating baritone sounded my name.

"Wiss, you jerk!"

I whirled at the familiar voice to stare into an unfamiliar face. It grinned conspiratorially at me.

"Alan! When'd you grow the 'stache?"

"Last night," the Shadow laughed, pulling me into the relative calm of a cul-de-sac. "How do you like the hair?" He tossed his salted and peppered locks with open fingers. "And the brows. Not bad, hey?"

"You look like a young Peter Lawford. What's it all for?"

He used his chin to point out two very well-attired middle-aged men chatting near the newsstand. "You see those two Suits? Their company sponsors a buddy of mine on the PBA circuit. There's a tourney in L.A. we're in, and they're going to check it out. So I scored a lift to the coast in the company jet."

"So today you're a pro bowler."

He smiled. "Call me Tommy."

"Okay, Alan."

"And what are *you* doing here? Coming or going?"

"Trying to go. My agent bungled my 'Frisco connection. I'll punish her when I get home; I'll have a game with her."

The Shadow brightened. "Then I've got a great idea! These Suits are bridge players. You could hitch with us to L.A. and we can get a game going. These guys won't mind and you can get to 'Frisco easy from there."

"You can stop twisting my arm anytime."

He caught the eye of one of the Suits, a stereotypically bald three-piecer sporting a large Havana and a paunch like a pumpkin under his vest. Waving at them with one hand, he tugged me along with the other.

"Just don't forget to call me Tommy," He reminded as we approached.

"Sure, Alan," I said.

*   *   *

An hour later we were high over Pennsylvania, winging it

westward, cutting for deal and partners in a friendly little one dollar game of Chicago. It need hardly be mentioned the Shadow was covering ninety per cent of my action.

The company copilot, who doubled as flight attendant/girl Friday, served us drinks and smiles and disappeared into the cockpit.

"You want another drink or anything, just push that button and she'll be right out," the Suit with the pumpkin paunch said.

"Thanks, I will," I said, cutting the Shadow as partner. I thought that was a good sign, but the cards were hardly friendly. Had my right hand Suit not ignored the vulnerability and walked into an eight hundred point set we would have been minus on the round. With little respect for either the scoring system or the dollar, they threw in overcalls with the frivolity of the penny players at the Regal in Toronto.

Other than bowling or bridge, there seemed to be little way to relate to the Suits in the moments of banter between hands. They had no interest in me and even less in discussing their company, or families, or golf game. Prudently, I suspect, I avoided any questions of the co-pilot. So much for trying to be polite.

On the following round I cut the Pumpkin for partner, with his stuffed shirt cohort on my right. They both took the reins of the same horse and pulled in opposite directions as Alan and I were reduced to powerless spectators.

I picked up: ♠AQxx ♡QT98xx ◇QTx ♣-. Stuffed Suit opened one club on my right. These Suits will open one club on a doubleton when holding a bad five card major, but on this hand it looked like clubs meant clubs. In spite of that, perhaps because of a perverse urge to go for Stuffed Suit's throat, I eschewed the overcall and doubled instead. After a pass by Alan and a quick pass by Pumpkin, S.S. ran to one heart! I knew what to do with that, thrilled I hadn't overcalled. After my double Pumpkin broke into a sweat. He tranced, he stewed, he extracted a handkerchief and wiped it over his pink pate. He banged his cards face down on the table.

"Six clubs!" he boomed.

"Double," said S.S., thumbing down the heart king before

anybody had a chance to redouble. Alan and I exchanged a
hapless glance as I tabled the dummy.

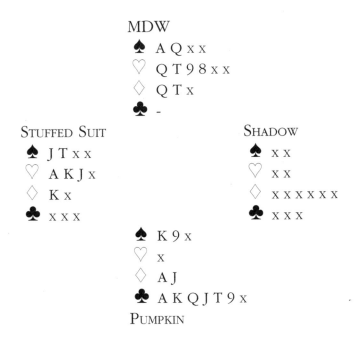

MDW
♠ A Q x x
♡ Q T 9 8 x x
♢ Q T x
♣ -

STUFFED SUIT
♠ J T x x
♡ A K J x
♢ K x
♣ x x x

SHADOW
♠ x x
♡ x x
♢ x x x x x x
♣ x x x

♠ K 9 x
♡ x
♢ A J
♣ A K Q J T 9 x
PUMPKIN

With every card marked on the bidding the hand is cold as
a shadow on the dark side of the moon. It virtually plays itself,
the count having been rectified at trick one. Simply win trick two
and run all the trumps to squeeze Stuffed Suit into submission.
It's not even necessary to cash the diamond ace early.

S.S. didn't want to put Pumpkin to the test, 'though. At trick
two he switched to his *fourth* best spade, and Pumpkin, seeing
no spade losers, forgot to count his winners and won the *king*
of spades! It was then inevitable that he drew the outstanding
trumps, tested spades (unlucky), and, thin-lipped and shrugging, took the diamond finesse. I chalked up my minus when
Pumpkin reminded me he had a hundred and fifty honours. O
Joy. Plus one hundred instead of plus ten ninety.

Pumpkin's dummy play improved on the next hand as he
made three notrump on a practice finesse, stretching our lead.
Then I had a small defensive problem.

SHADOW	S.S.		S.S.
1 ♠	2 ♣		♠ J x
3 ♣	3 ♥		♡ A x
4 ♡	4 ♠		◇ Q T x x
5 ◇	5 ♥		♣ K Q 9 x x
6 ♠	P		

♠ A T
♡ x x x
◇ K x x x
♣ x x x x

MDW

Pumpkin led the ace of diamonds. Alan ruffed and led a spade to the jack and my ace. Now what?

I reflected on the bidding. Why S.S. didn't bid three diamonds rather than three hearts was beyond me, but then bidding of that nature usually is. Alan appeared to be 5-4-0-4. Which meant Pumpkin had no clubs. Further, Pumpkin would likely have led a stiff club if he had one. I confess if I didn't own the king of diamonds I may have given the hand more thought. Vaguely I wondered why Alan hadn't tried to ruff a heart. I put a club on the track.

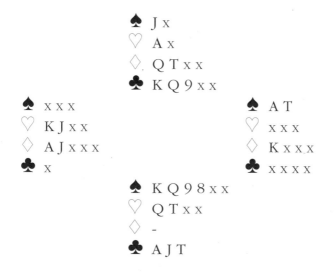

♠ J x
♡ A x
◇ Q T x x
♣ K Q 9 x x

♠ x x x   ♠ A T
♡ K J x x   ♡ x x x
◇ A J x x x   ◇ K x x x
♣ x   ♣ x x x x

♠ K Q 9 8 x x
♡ Q T x x
◇ -
♣ A J T

Alan's ace disappointingly held the trick. Both the Pumpkin and I had missed our chances to beat the slam.

Alan drew trumps, careful to pitch a heart from dummy, then overtook a club to lead the diamond queen. Since both Suits lead king from ace-king, I knew that he knew I held the king, so I was forced to cover. He ruffed, overtook his last club, and ran the suit to produce this ending:

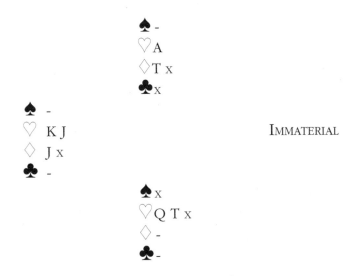

On the last club Alan pitched a heart and Pumpkin squirmed. A trump transfer squeeze with a criss-cross overtone.

"*Nice* play, Tommy," I muttered under Stuffed Suit's laughter. "I could have busted it up with a heart but..."

"How could you have known? You made a good play," he said graciously.

"I could use another drink," I said, and thumbed the call button. The angel of the air appeared.

"Refills, gentlemen?" she said, smiling. And making wonderful eye contact, I noticed.

"What's your name?" I asked.

"Co-captain O'Hara," she said, heading for the galley. Pumpkin guffawed.

"You've got a better chance stepping outside and walking than you have with her," he said when she was out of earshot.

A few hours and many hands later we heard the whine of the engines soften and felt the plane start to descend.

"Last hand," said Pumpkin, who had wound up across from me again. "We're coming in soon. Let's triple the stakes." Since I was up forty points by then and the Shadow twice that, we could hardly refuse.

Pumpkin dealt the cards, and we promptly passed it out.

"Let's ghoulie it!" Pumpkin chimed. Sure. Why not?

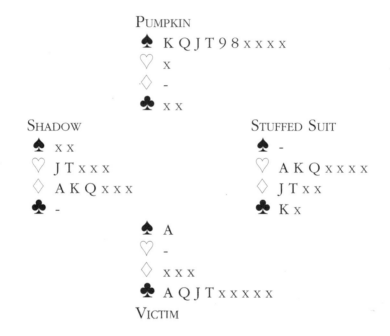

PUMPKIN
♠ K Q J T 9 8 x x x x
♡ x
♢ -
♣ x x

SHADOW
♠ x x
♡ J T x x x
♢ A K Q x x x
♣ -

STUFFED SUIT
♠ -
♡ A K Q x x x x
♢ J T x x
♣ K x

♠ A
♡ -
♢ x x x
♣ A Q J T x x x x x
VICTIM

A typical ghoulie, and consistent with my theory that ghoulies should be bid using transfer openings, with one notrump a transfer to Stayman. Grand slams in diamonds, hearts, and spades are all cold, but only from the *short* side. Switch the spade ace and king to submarine the blockage and the club grand also makes. From the short side.

Alan opened one diamond and Pumpkin lost no time in bidding game in spades. Stuffed Suit bid five diamonds, after a moment's thought, and it wasn't too hard for me to work out where all the hearts went on this deal. I wanted to bid six spades, but I was sure they wouldn't let me buy the hand. Five was enough. When it got around to S.S. he thought his hand worth another call and bid the diamond slam. Now when I bid six spades Alan doubled, looking for an unusual lead. It wasn't long in coming. S.S. led the heart king.

Not wishing to waste his trump ace, and having once, I'm sure, heard of an expert play called a loser-on-loser, Pumpkin pitched a diamond from dummy in order to stake everything on the club finesse. S.S. noticed the Shadow's heart deuce at trick one, and divined to switch to the club deuce. After much torture, both to self and, I assure you, dummy, Pumpkin backed his original line and took the finesse, which duly worked.

Sort of.

I retired to the executive washroom for a little break. When I returned Alan suggested I take up bowling.

Not too long afterwards we were on the tarmac, shaking hands near the nose of the Lear.

"Do you need a lift into town?" Pumpkin asked me.

"No, thanks. I'm going up to San Francisco. I'm just going inside to check on the next flight."

"San Francisco! Why didn't you say so? That's where our head offices are. The jet's leaving empty right now. You just go on and climb right back on board!" So I did.

I shook Alan's hand last. "Later,Tommy. Next time; next place."

"'Until that time, Eustus'," he smiled.

I turned up the steps of the jet. Co-captain O'Hara was standing there, her hand extended to help me aboard.

"Welcome back," she said. "I'm Liz."

Shadow in the Zone

IT HAPPENS TO THE BEST; IT HAPPENS TO the worst.

To the worst, all finesses work, all seven-card fits break three-three, and all second-best contracts come home when the first would have failed. To the best, the cards dance. They lie favourably for the exotic squeeze, the cunning deception, and the never-quite-hopelessly overbid.

In both cases, the opponents invariably find their worst possible leads and switches.

It's called being "in the 'Zone'", and is a phenomenon common not just to bridge players, but to participants in any sport imaginable. When you're 'Zoning', *everything* works.

* * *

The Shadow and I drifted into Cavendish West on one of the smoggiest days in known history, the haze of sky diarrhoea in the L.A. basin odiously umber and acidic. It was a pleasure to get my stinging and tearing eyes into the air-conditioned coolness of the club, where the smoke from pipe, cigar, and cigarette was a mild joke compared to the outside air.

While the Shadow sought some fortune at the backgammon tables I slid into a two-penny Chicago graced with none other than Don Adams of 'Get Smart' notoriety, who soon proved himself no slouch with the cards. Had his Maxwell Smart character played bridge, there's little doubt he would be a lucksack rabbit who would emerge unscratched every time he hopped into the briar patch. His real persona was clearly more bacon than bunny.

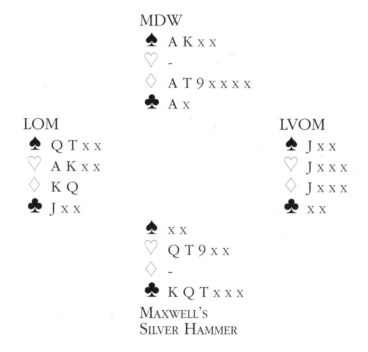

MDW
♠ A K x x
♡ -
♢ A T 9 x x x x
♣ A x

LOM
♠ Q T x x
♡ A K x x
♢ K Q
♣ J x x

LVOM
♠ J x x
♡ J x x x
♢ J x x x
♣ x x

♠ x x
♡ Q T 9 x x
♢ -
♣ K Q T x x x

Maxwell's
Silver Hammer

I dealt with all vulnerable, opening one diamond. With the opponents, a little old man and a little very old man, blessedly silent for the first time in the set, Don responded one heart. I rebid one spade, and Don trotted out the club suit. I jumped to three diamonds, expecting to hear three no trump, but Don rebid his clubs. I mentally shrugged and raised to the club game. The LOM led the king of hearts.

Playing quickly and competently Don ruffed the heart, ruffed a diamond, led a trump to the ace and ruffed another diamond. The king and queen drew the outstanding trumps, on which two spades in dummy were tossed. Dummy was entered with a spade, and when the ace of diamonds failed to split the balance Don simply ruffed another with his last trump, and claimed, the last diamonds in dummy now high and the spade entry remaining.

"Thanks, pard," I said. "Well stroked."

At that moment the Shadow slipped up behind me.

"There's a hole open in Meyer Schliefer's game," he said. "I'll be there whenever you want to drift over."

"Save me a seat; I'll be there after this set."

Except by the time I'd cut out and pulled up beside Alan, Meyer had already left, and I got deprived of the pleasure of watching Schliefer and the Shadow in the same game. Drat.

On the other hand, my presence was timely, for the Shadow was just then entering the Zone.

First, a small defensive problem. On first deal you pick up: ♠Kxxx ♡AKTxxx ◇- ♣AQx. A nice little mitt. Right hand opponent opens with six diamonds! Do you double? If so, you lead. Top heart? Or because this is a lead problem do you lead a heart only at the table? An attacking spade? A speculative club?

Alan's LHO, a gaunt and swarthy fellow in his forties with a five o'clock shadow at high noon, did double and did lead a top heart.

When is ace from ace-queen better than ace from ace-king? I wondered. Other than this time, of course.

THE GREMLIN
♠ Q T x x x x
♡ x x x
♢ -
♣ J T x x

SWARTHY FELLOW
♠ K x x x
♡ A K T x x x
♢ -
♣ A Q x

STUNT MAN
♠ x
♡ Q J x x
♢ x x x
♣ x x x x x

♠ A x
♡ -
♢ A K Q J T 9 x x x x
♣ K

THE SHADOW

The play was over quickly. Alan simply ruffed and ran all his trumps, strip-squeezing S.F. down to three cards. S.F. saw what was coming, to give him credit, and after unloading his hearts he pitched all three of his little spades before letting go his baby club. Unfortunately for him he wasn't able to avoid the slightest hitch before releasing the last spade.

Alan's antennae were fully extended, and reading the position he slipped his baby spade into his breast pocket, leaving half the back exposed like a cardboard hankie, and placed the spade ace and club king face down on the table. He passed the cards back and forth over each other like a street hustler with a pea game, waggled a finger as he eenie-meenied between them, and before the disbelieving eyes of both S.F. and the Stunt Man flipped over the ace of spades.

"You lucky S.O.B.!" he exclaimed, as Alan smiled and extracted the baby spade from his pocket. Plus fifteen-forty.

"Why the hell didn't you bid six hearts?" S.F. berated the Stunt Man.

"Because it doesn't make," he retorted. "Just like six diamonds doesn't if you lead the ace of clubs!"

Alan snuck a sly grin at me over his shoulder as S.F. dealt the next hand.

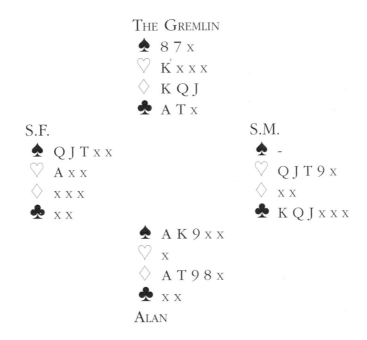

THE GREMLIN
♠ 8 7 x
♡ K x x x
♢ K Q J
♣ A T x

S.F.
♠ Q J T x x
♡ A x x
♢ x x x
♣ x x

S.M.
♠ -
♡ Q J T 9 x
♢ x x
♣ K Q J x x x

♠ A K 9 x x
♡ x
♢ A T 9 8 x
♣ x x

ALAN

The Swarthy Fellow grunted and passed, still displeased with the previous hand. The Shadow's partner, a very small gremlin-like man on the shady side of a half century, opened one club, causing the out-of-work stunt man to hitch long enough to talk himself into overcalling one heart. Alan bid one spade, S.F. passed contentedly, and the Gremlin bid one no trump. Stunt Man decided now was the time to bid his real suit, and called two clubs. Alan jumped to three diamonds and the Gremlin quietly preferred three spades. Alan raised himself to game and S.F. came to life with a double that, had bidding boxes been in vogue in those days, would have seen all the red cards available float to the top of the table.

Unfortunately for him, he chose to lead the stunt man's first bid suit instead of his second, and placed the heart ace on the table, switching quickly to a club once he saw the dummy.

Alan won the ace and shed his other club on the heart king. Then he ruffed a club, entered dummy with a diamond, and ruffed a heart back to hand. A diamond to dummy and a diamond back, overtaking the last honour, left this position:

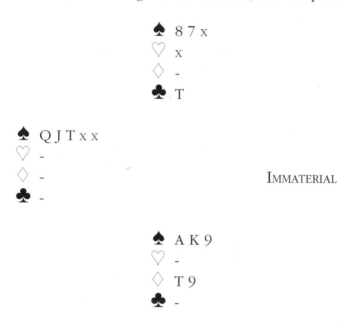

♠ 8 7 x
♡ x
◇ -
♣ T

♠ Q J T x x
♡ -
◇ -   IMMATERIAL
♣ -

♠ A K 9
♡ -
◇ T 9
♣ -

Alan put the Curse of Scotland on the table and S.F. was diddled. He ruffed with the ten and returned the queen, but Alan won and played the diamond ten, showing his remaining cards.

"Dammit!" S.F. griped.

"Good of you to expose the trump position," Stunt Man said.

"Good of *you* to bid twice on air!" S.F. retorted.

A few deals later the Shadow partnered the Stunt Man with the Gremlin on his right. At unfavourable vulnerability he picked up: ♠Ax ♡A9xx ◇xx ♣AKQTx, opening one club. With S.F. and the Gremlin silent throughout the Stunt Man responded two diamonds. Two hearts collected two spades and Alan stalled with two no trump, allowing the Stunt Man to clarify his hand. In his own roundabout fashion he proceeded to do so, first calling three diamonds, presumably promising a solid suit at least six long. Alan cued the spade ace and heard four hearts, presumably a king cue, and probably denying the spade king, else by now he would have launched into Blackwood. Alan bid five clubs, confirming the ace and value concentration, and sending the Stunt Man into the tank. After a few moments he emerged with a firm five hearts.

Alan told me later that it was at this very point, the Binsky burp of the Stunted One (as we came to later refer to him, since it was apparent he had fallen off one horse too many), that it first occurred to him that the wheels might have come off.

Could S.O. now be cueing the heart queen? If so, Alan could count thirteen tricks and should now bid a grand in no trump. Could he have a singleton king and be showing a third-round control? No, then he should already have placed the contract in slam of one minor or the other. Maybe he's bidding his shape, and is 4-3-6-0 and was afraid to bid the club void for fear he would be showing support.

Deciding finally in favour of prudence Alan bid a simple six diamonds, which rated to be a plus no matter what had happened.

Except the Stunted One now bid six hearts(!), and Alan passed. The choice between the wheels having come off and the Stunted One now showing fourth-round heart control was not difficult to make.

The Swarthy Fellow led the ten of diamonds and the Shadow silently surveyed the dummy for a *long* time.

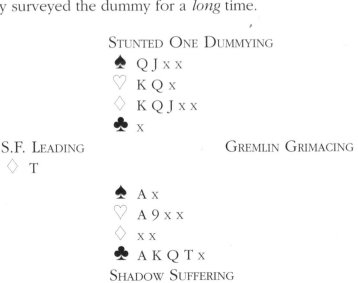

STUNTED ONE DUMMYING

♠ Q J x x
♡ K Q x
◇ K Q J x x
♣ x

S.F. LEADING   GREMLIN GRIMACING
◇ T

♠ A x
♡ A 9 x x
◇ x x
♣ A K Q T x
SHADOW SUFFERING

Ah, yes. The 'I have an opening hand, too' variety of the jump shift. Knowing Alan as I do I know he was spending half the time at trick one calming himself to enable him to concentrate on the job at hand. When he began scratching an ear I knew he'd begun thinking about the hand and not about the top ten ways to ensure the demise of his partner.

The lead went to the jack and Gremlin's ace, and the suit was returned, won perforce in the dummy. The spade finesse was needed; that was a certainty. But then what? Ruff a club and play hearts to be three-three? Against the percentages. Take a club finesse? Play clubs to be 4-3 and the jack to drop? Against the percentages. I could see the Shadow's gears grinding. He floated the queen of spades when the Gremlin followed low. It worked.

He cashed the king and queen of hearts, on which S.F. deposited the jack. Finally some percentage in favour. He played a heart to the nine, and S.F. tossed a spade. The ace drew the last trump, and the third top club dropped the jack from the Gremlin. It was both onside *and* third. Plus fourteen thirty. Now I knew why the Gremlin had been grimacing.

The Shadow turned to look at me, a beatific expression on his face.

"I guess we had to play in clubs to score the honours," he said.

Later the Shadow partnered the Swarthy Fellow, and showed he had yet to leave cruising altitude in the Zone. The Gremlin opened one spade on Alan's right, and Alan overcalled one no trump holding: ♠AK9 ♡K8xxx ◇xx ♣KQx. The Stunted One came in with two clubs, and the Swarthy Fellow, in generous praise to Alan's earlier heroics, bid three diamonds. Alan tried the no trump game. In the Zone everything works.

SWARTHY
♠ J T x
♡ 9
◇ K J x x x x x
♣ x x

The Stunt Man led a low club to the Gremlin's jack. The Shadow played low in tempo as I blinked. It took me a moment to realise what a fine play he had made.

STUNTED ONE	GREMLIN
♠ Q	♠ 8 x x x x x
♡ J T x x	♡ A Q x
◇ Q 9	◇ A T
♣ A T 8 x x x	♣ J 9

It was clear a heart switch would beat the contract at least two tricks at this point, but, perhaps as bemused as we all were at the sight of the dummy, the Gremlin continued clubs. The Stunt Man won and cleared the suit, Alan tossing a diamond from dummy, the Gremlin pitching a spade. In hand, Alan led a diamond to the jack, which held the trick. The spade jack back wasn't covered, but when Alan overtook it the lady came tumbling on his left! Another diamond cleared the suit, and the heart ace was the last trick for the defense.

"Thanks, pard," the Swarthy Fellow said.

"O, think nothing of it," Alan said, biting his lip. Later he told me if the spade queen hadn't appeared he would have played the Gremlin for AQJ frozen of hearts, eventually forcing him to provide a stepping stone to dummy. Of course in the Zone the spade queen and heart jack are in the same hand.

The Gremlin was bemoaning his fate. "I could have switched to a heart at trick two and beaten it. Or *you* could have led a heart, on the other hand."

"Good thing I didn't lead the suit you bid," the Stunt Man countered. "He'd have made an overtrick."

The last hand of the set found Alan dealing, with he and the Swarthy Fellow having a forty leg on.

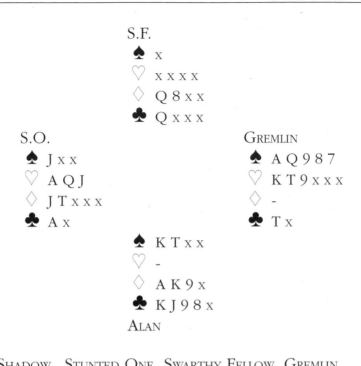

S.F.
♠ x
♡ x x x x
♢ Q 8 x x
♣ Q x x x

S.O.
♠ J x x
♡ A Q J
♢ J T x x x
♣ A x

GREMLIN
♠ A Q 9 8 7
♡ K T 9 x x x
♢ -
♣ T x

♠ K T x x
♡ -
♢ A K 9 x
♣ K J 9 8 x
ALAN

SHADOW	STUNTED ONE	SWARTHY FELLOW	GREMLIN
1 ♣	1 ♢	2 ♣	3 ♣
3 ♢	4 ♣	4 ♢	4 ♡
5 ♣	5 ♡	P	P
DBL.	P	P	P

Everybody took turns cuebidding each other's suits until the Stunted One yet again burped out Binsky. By then the Shadow had heard more than enough. He put the boots to the contract and led a top diamond.

When you're in the Zone, the opponent's cold contracts somehow go down. The Gremlin ruffed the opening lead and led a trump to the dummy, none too pleased when Alan showed out, pitching the Curse of Ireland. At this point the Gremlin could have drawn trumps and floated the seven of spades from hand. Considering the apparent shape of Alan's hand it would seem the indicated play. Not being anywhere near a Zone, however, he drew only three rounds of trumps and played a low spade to the queen. Alan was quick to win and return the suit, following the first bridge rule of Confucius - 'Both sides play same suit, one side clazy!'. The Swarthy Fellow ruffed gratefully and the setting trick came along in due course.

"I've had enough of this!" the Gremlin groaned, throwing down his cards and rising from his chair. "Cut me out. I knew I should have gone to the goddam track."

"You in?" S.O. said to me.

"No chancey," I said.

"A good time to call it quits," Alan agreed as we stood together. "I feel like an old-fashioned burger at the Hamlet."

* * *

While the Shadow was collecting his winnings I stood by the door, watching Maxwell sling his silver hammer. It was clear he was enjoying himself. Glancing up, he tossed me a grin and a wave.

The Shadow and I stepped out of the Zone and into the smog.

Shadow Pairing

IT WAS BOUND TO HAPPEN. SOONER OR later the Shadow had to show up in town - in what guise I had no inkle - with the discovery that I had been penning quiet little tales of his many and varied exploits.

I was living in Toronto at the time, with one of my favourite wives who to this day and forever remains one of my closest friends. It was well past two in the ayem when Hap's bark and Bunch's elbow simultaneously informed me the phone was ringing. Roslyn dislikes answering phones, or bells of any kind. This probably explains why she's a teacher, and why, in a domestic application of Murphy's Law, the telephone rested on *her* night table. I rolled over, reached over, and garbled something into the earpiece.

"Wiss, you jerk!" the earpiece spoke back. I turned it around. "Where do you get off writing about me?"

"Alan! How are you? *Where* are you?" Clever ethnic tactic that nowadays is getting around...answer a question with a question.

"Ottawa. In a hotel. Reading something called *The Kibitzer*. Now stuff your clever ethnic tactics and answer me. Is this a test of our friendship?"

"Who is it?" Roslyn mumbled.

"A Shadow in the night. Go back to sleep."

"The hell I will," the phone spoke back. "The bar's closed and I've had a half dozen scotches waiting until I knew *you* were asleep before I called."

"Alan, you always said you wanted to be anonymous. So you're anonymous. I've been careful, haven't I?"

"If you blow my cover, Wiss, you're disinherited. I mean it."

"What do you have me down for?"

"My plastic playing cards and all my golf balls."

"In that case I'll behave - if you promise to predecease me, that is."

"I promise nothing. Moreover, I may add a codicil and subtract your balls, just for the hell of it."

"Alan, I'm tired."

"All right, all right... I'll be in Toronto tomorrow. I'm free in the evening. What are you up to?"

"Sorry to say, I'm working late. Won't be home till ten."

"In that case give your lovely wife my regrets, since I won't see her, and set me up for a pairs game."

"Pairs? Are you kidding?"

"Nope. The people I'll be seeing earlier like to drink a bit. I'll be in no shape for rubber at the Regal. It's not clear I'll be in any shape for pairs at Horning's either, but what the hay?"

"You can play with the Bunch." The 'Bunch' was my wife. She had acquired her sobriquet at the bridge table. Whenever she 'goofed' she would exclaim: 'O, what a banana I am!', sometimes punctuating the statement with a quick smack to her forehead. Since none of us are capable of error-free sessions, it is apparent that a goof rears its ugly head on numerous occasions in the course of over two dozen hands. Bananas, naturally, come in bunches.

"Veto," Alan said. "For the same reason I won't play with you in Toronto. Somebody who can count to thirteen might put together two and two."

"You're being paranoid. Just come as yourself, the bridge world self, I mean. People'd just think you're in town for a visit, which you are."

"It's a thought. Who do you know that plays EHAA?"

"Half the city. Or do you want someone who can follow suit as well?"

"That'd be a nice change."

"I'll get you Gowdy. He appreciates entertainment much as you do, and if none around creates it. And I'm still tired. Call me at work and I'll let you know what's happening. G'night now." I hung up.

Gowdy was unavailable, but I found the Shadow a suitable, if dissimilar, replacement. Swearing his partner to secrecy - not that anyone would believe him anyway - was perhaps secondary to the threat of calling in his IOU's, which have never been insignificant. I left Alan to garner his giggles where he may, with little fear that he would miss many. When he's had an extra drink with dinner he goes after laughs like a hog rooting for truffles.

I rolled in midway through the session, helped myself to a coffee, and discreetly kibitzed the Shadow's nameless partner. My timing was impeccable. They were about to begin a three board round against Gloria and Beatrice, two venerable and proper Little Old Ladies known around the club as Glory Be, who were capable of manipulating the cards in manners never dreamed.

Of course, Alan didn't know that.

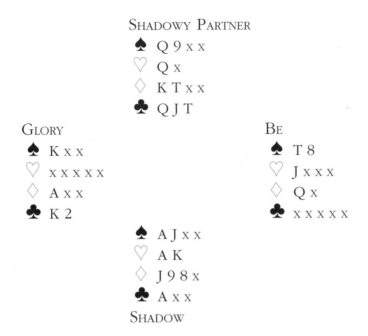

SHADOWY PARTNER
♠ Q 9 x x
♡ Q x
◇ K T x x
♣ Q J T

GLORY
♠ K x x
♡ x x x x x
◇ A x x
♣ K 2

BE
♠ T 8
♡ J x x x
◇ Q x
♣ x x x x x

♠ A J x x
♡ A K
◇ J 9 8 x
♣ A x x
SHADOW

The Shadow quickly got to game in spades. Glory, however, aware her LHO was a well-known local player, and her RHO someone whose face she probably saw in the Bulletin before, and an LHK who had just settled and was watching her every move, did not choose her lead so quickly. She fingered her fourth best heart, then her top heart, then a small spade, and finally the LOL Standby Fave, the king of clubs.

Realising she was taking everybody else's time along with her own, she snatched at her last choice, catching instead the card adjacent. In a moment the deuce of clubs(!) was on the table and Alan was thoughtfully studying the dummy.

What was the deuce lead? Surely no singleton after all that thought. And not from the king into the teeth of a notrump opener. That left three or four small. So, if the diamond queen were onside and spades friendly - singleton or doubleton king on, or dubby ten off - twelve tricks were there.

Shrugging, Alan won the lead in dummy and played a spade to the jack. Glory won the king and put a low diamond down. Alan looked at it a moment and, as would you or I, ducked. Be won the queen and thought about things, then, as partners sometimes will, returned her partner's *original* suit. Was it diabolical greed? Well, I know. But I'm not telling.

Alan, of course, ducked again. Glory won the king, cashed the ace of diamonds, gave Be a diamond ruff, and got a club ruff coming home. Minus three hundred.

Alan looked up at me with the same expression Roberto de Vicenzo must have worn when informed he'd just signed an incorrect scorecard at the Master's.

"Happy Halloween," I said.

Then arrived:

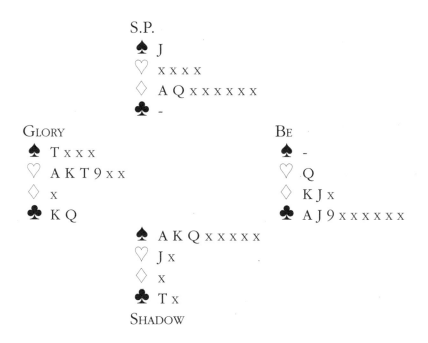

In first seat the Shadow decided to gamble out three notrump, which bought the hand. This time Glory had no trouble with her lead. She tabled the king of hearts, non-attitude, looked at Be's queen, and played a low heart! Betraying a slight smile, Alan won his jack, laid down the ace of spades, and wiped off the smile. He then tried to make the hand, cashing two more spades and taking the diamond hook, hoping for king and another onside. The resulting Miami Endplay was good for down five.

"Do you suppose anyone bid a rounded slam their way?" Alan's partner asked me quietly.

"The queen is supposed to show the jack," Glory reminded Be.

The last hand gave the Shadow an opportunity to salvage a few matchpoints from the round. He held at unfavourable vulnerability: ♠Jxx ♡Jxx ◇x ♣T98xxx and heard Glory's opening two notrump get passed around to him. In tempo he bid three clubs, which his partner promptly alerted.

"Ye-es?" Glory said.

"He has an unspecified one-suiter."

"In clubs?"

Alan smiled. "Possibly," he said patiently. "I must bid three diamonds, and he then bids his suit."

"What if it's diamonds?"

"Then he'll either pass or raise."

"O. In that case I'll pass."

When Be doubled the 'automatic' three diamond call the Shadow 'ran' to four clubs.

"Now I double," Glory said.

This was the entire hand:

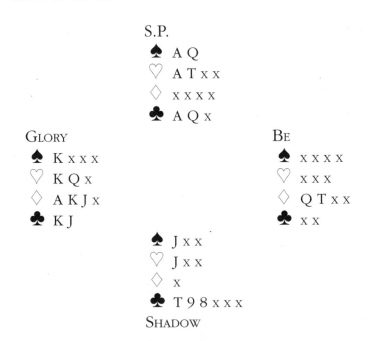

S.P.
♠ A Q
♡ A T x x
◇ x x x x
♣ A Q x

GLORY
♠ K x x x
♡ K Q x
◇ A K J x
♣ K J

BE
♠ x x x x
♡ x x x
◇ Q T x x
♣ x x

♠ J x x
♡ J x x
◇ x
♣ T 9 8 x x x
SHADOW

Glory led the king of diamonds, and followed it with the ace. Alan ruffed, drew trumps with the finesse, ruffed himself to hand, hooked the spade, cashed the spade ace, ruffed another diamond and ruffed his last spade. He then played a heart to his jack and Glory's queen and claimed the balance on the marked heart finesse. Plus nine-ten. The entire play took about twenty seconds.

We stepped into the hall while waiting for the next round to be called. "My hand was bad enough to be good," Alan said. "Does anyone defend two notrump undoubled anymore?"

"Other than what I just witnessed, how are you two doing?" I asked.

"If we fail to make it as bridge players, there's also the national Yo-Yo championship. Otherwise we're doomed to repairing elevators. That last round was pretty indicative of the entire game. Adventureland in there. The hesitations and voice tones are incredible."

"There's a positive side," S.P. said. "You can't misguess a two-way hook for a queen."

"Let's test your table feel, Mikey. Twice tonight I've held king-jack fifth in dummy and two pups in hand. On the first one you lead up and the lady on your left ducks smoothly. Which card do you play?"

"I go into the tank," I stalled. Another clever tactic. "What do my opponents do?"

"I thought you'd ask. LHO sits stiff as a board..."

"Aha! Clue one; acting like she's hiding something."

"...and when you glance under the table RHO is tapping a foot."

"Clue two; impatience confirming clue one. I tell partner to play whichever honour he wants from the dummy - they're both offside!"

Alan laughed. "That was an easy one. Part bee is tougher. This time LHO tanks for close to ten seconds before winning the ace, then breaks a side suit of ace and empties."

"Looks like AQx onside. Do I need pitches, where I might have to hook the jack?"

"Nope. But say you need a safe way back to hand to draw trumps."

"Then I cash the king and..."

"LHO ruffs." S.P. was chuckling.

"Pardon me?"

"Yup. Really happened. LHO couldn't quite convince the police she was thinking about what to switch to when she won her stiff ace. This is a tough game you got me into."

"*I* got you into?"

*　*　*

Little of interest occurred over the next two rounds. An owl-like person bid a hog-like slam needing a rabbit-like piece of luck. A hook with a three-three break and a squeeze. No problem. The Shadow placed a shrugging zero on his scorecard and quiet averages, give or take, on the other five boards.

Then came the last round, placing on the Shadow's left a well-known worm-like fellow with table presence considerably better than the average earthworm. A quiet demeanor belied a competitive nature willing to keep ears, and eyes, open for any advantage. Some consider him a blood brother of Charlie the Chimp.

This was the first hand:

S.P.
♠ Q 7 x
♡ A x
♢ x x x
♣ K T 9 8 x

THE WORM
♠ A J 8
♡ Q x x
♢ K T x x
♣ Q J x

THE WORM'S WABBIT
♠ K x x
♡ J x x x
♢ Q J x x
♣ x x

♠ T 9 x x
♡ K T x x
♢ A x
♣ A 7 x
THE SHADOW

W.W.	SHADOW	WORM	S.P.
P	1 ♣	P?	2 ♣
P	P	DBL	P
2 ♡	P	P	3 ♣
P	P	DBL?	P
P	P		

The bidding requires some explanation, not entirely due to the fact that the board had been turned around, placing Alan in second seat rather than fourth, as he should have been. After Alan had opened, the Worm fumbled and twitched and said aloud, "I, uh, found another card." Pause. Insert. "Pa-ass?" I refrained from rolling my eyes. Sometimes it's *tough* to kibitz. When the Worm's last double came in the same tone of voice as his first pass, Alan had great difficulty refraining from rolling his. Well, he failed, if you're going to twist my arm over it.

The deuce of hearts opening lead must have been a gift of Lady Justice peeking uncharacteristically from beneath her blindfold. Left to his own devices Alan would sooner or later have to break spades himself, going set a trick. Now he was able to set up the heart ten with a third round ruff for trick number nine. Plus six seventy, thank you very much.

"Tough game," the Shadow said.

The next board was in the proper direction, placing the Shadow in his favourite position. He gave us an entertaining demonstration of what he called the 'prop-ah' use of a popular convention. It's not clear just what Mr. Drury would have thought of it, but nobody dreams up a convention with an eye towards the tactical uses for which it may be employed.

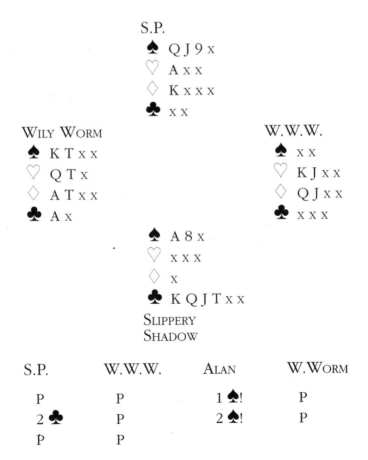

S.P.
♠ Q J 9 x
♡ A x x
◇ K x x x
♣ x x

WILY WORM
♠ K T x x
♡ Q T x
◇ A T x x
♣ A x

W.W.W.
♠ x x
♡ K J x x
◇ Q J x x
♣ x x x

♠ A 8 x
♡ x x x
◇ x
♣ K Q J T x x

SLIPPERY
SHADOW

S.P.	W.W.W.	ALAN	W. WORM
P	P	1 ♣!	P
2 ♣	P	2 ♠!	P
P	P		

They were playing a form of the convention wherein only the rebid of the original suit showed a light opener, all other calls being constructive and descriptive, and showing full values.

Where the Shadow found his one spade opener only he and Adam Meredith know, and it's rumoured The Plum isn't talking. Lesser practitioners of the convention might pass the Drury two club bid, but knowing this only leads to a virtual automatic balance by the Worm, Alan *rebid* his three card suit!

"And why not?" he said later. "A major Moysian at matchpoints with ruffs in the short hand, and a good side suit; what could be better?" With one-ten to one-forty common the other way, plus one-forty was worth approximately sixteen matchpoints out of eight. I credited the Worm with suffering his ignominy in silence.

Whereupon came the evening's final treat:

	S.P.	
	♠ K 2	
	♡ A	
	◇ Q T x 2	
	♣ A J 9 8 x 2	

THE WORM		W.W.
♠ Q x x x		♠ J x x x
♡ x x x x		♡ Q T x x
◇ A K x x x		◇ x
♣ -		♣ Q x x x

	♠ A T x	
	♡ K J 9 x	
	◇ J x x	
	♣ K T 7	
	ALAN	

W.W.	ALAN	WORM	S.P.
P	P	1 ◇	2 ♣
P	2 ◇	P	3 ◇
P	3NT	P	P
P			

The Worm led a top diamond and switched quickly to a heart. The Shadow surveyed the dummy, and after a few moments I noticed the trace of a smile. He called for dummy's third best club, the Curse of Ireland, and overtook it with the ten. When the Worm pitched a heart Alan fired up his last low diamond. The Worm glanced at the ten in dummy and ducked. Oops.

Normally Alan would have claimed at this point, but, perversely perhaps, he played it out. Winning the diamond ten in dummy he led his second worst club to the seven, cashed his rounded kings, pitching the queen of diamonds, played a spade to the king, and cashed clubs from the top down arriving at this pretty ending:

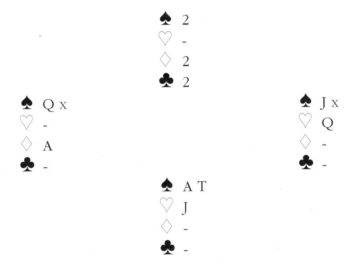

On the lead of the lowest club W.W. had to throw a spade to retain the queen of hearts, Alan followed with his now useless heart jack, and the worm squirmed. Plus four-ninety was worth about sixty-four out of eight matchpoints. The last round had squeaked the Shadow and his partner into the overalls.

*   *   *

"Matchpoints," the Shadow muttered later over his third vodka neat, "the bane of my sanity. It's beyond me why I continue to indulge in these flights of self-flagellation."

"It's a shame psychiatry isn't one of your fields of interest."

"By my definition, at least, it's not a sport. Wiss, I don't want to read about tonight. And if I ever have to wake you up again at two ayem..."

I crossed my legs. Inside the softness of my Bruno Maglis I crossed my toes. Turning my head, I crossed my eyes.

"Don't worry," I promised. "I'll never write another word about you."

Shadow in the Bible Belt

ARRIVING IN MINNEAPOLIS, OR ANY-
where else for that matter, at five-
fifteen in the morning after twenty-
four hours in the coach seating of
assorted trains, is an experience to
wish only on an enemy.

I stepped from the train, un-
washed, bleary-eyed, groggier than a crab after a rice
wine swim. At such times it's good to have friends.

As I struggled up the lobby ramp carrying a bag that
appeared ten kilos heavier than when I left Saskatoon,
I saw Patrick waiting at the top, one hand extended for
my bag, the other for a squeeze on my shoulder as we
greeted. The bag left my grip like a featherweight as his
giant paw settled, then patted.

"Ribbit," he said, referring to an equally late night of
the past, when we shared a time of lifelong remem-
brance under a full moon while walking on a deserted
branch highway thirty miles south of the city. I laughed
through my exhaustion and gave him a hug.

"Jeez, am I glad to be here," I breathed.

"I have a chauffeured limousine outside and a pick-me-up prepared," he said, ushering me to the door. He led me to the corner where he stopped beside a twenty-two ton garbage truck, waiting with an impish grin on his face until realisation tired of trying to break through the titanium of my skull and finally slipped into my somnambulistic consciousness through my ears. I jerked a thumb at the truck and broke into a fit of escalating giggling as he nodded. Exhaustion causes people to do odd things.

"Chauffeur?" I choked out, pointing at Patrick. My laughter was contagious. As his gorilla-like torso heaved in amusement he nodded and held open the passenger door for me. In my condition it was like scaling a cliff. I settled into the cab and noticed the pick-me-up jammed into the top crack of the glove box adjacent to a wooden match.

Patrick thinks of everything.

We spent a pleasant four hours on a tour of the back alleys of the Bible Belt as I accompanied him on his rounds. After a trip to the dump outside the city we returned to his home where I napped, washed, and refuelled. Then we hopped on his Harley, a fifteen hundred c.c. moose, and he whisked me downtown to the Raddison where the regional was being held. I had a date to meet the Shadow for lunch before kibitzing him in a pairs game with one of his favourite clients, a blue-haired born-in-the-bush Bible Belter whom he affectionately referred to as the Piranha Lady, for her willingness to take a piece out of any opponent unwise enough either to underestimate or to ignore her.

I found them both waiting in the lobby, Alan pointing at a convention card in his hand and the Piranha Lady puffing expansively on a cigarette jammed crooked into an eight-inch rhinestone-adorned holder.

In those days smoking was still allowed on the tournament floor, monkeypoints were awarded by the cup and not the bushel, and I was a thirty-year-old novice eager to improve my play.

"Mikey!" Alan greeted, standing to shake my hand as I

approached. "Glad you made it. This is Lydia, one of my favourite partners and favourite people in the world."

Lydia was slim and sixtyish, stylishly attired, and carefully coiffed. Her bright blue eyes, complementing the azure tinge of her hair, twinkled over the reading glasses perched precariously on the end of her nose. She shook my hand and smiled.

"Alan's told me everything bad about you," she started.

"Well, then," I said, "I guess I'm safe from bites."

"Only if we're not at the table," she answered.

"I knew you two would hit it off," Alan said. "What say we get some lunch?"

Over soup I listened intently, as for the most part the conversation was centred on the continued discussion of their convention card. Since Lydia was a life master three times over and I a non-LM three times under, I thought it would behoove me to follow the number one kibitzer rule of E.O.E.O.M.S., namely Eyes Open, Ears Open, Mouth Shut. Inevitably I could learn something.

What I learned was that Lydia was a professional's dream client. She was intelligent, a good listener, and not afraid to question. At the table she was competent, attentive, and aggressive. Not that it mattered to Alan, she was both generous, and wealthy. What *did* matter was that she had a great sense of humour, a bleeding raw wit, and a *sans souci* attitude.

The very first round bore evidence to all. Two serious young men were already seated in the east-west chairs as Alan and Lydia took their places north-south and I pulled up a chair beside Alan. They were engrossed in a quietly heated disagreement over nothing particularly important.

"Good afternoon, young gentlemen," Lydia greeted as she placed her coffee cup on the table and sat down. The fellow on her left, resplendent in hippie brown, merely grunted as he glanced at her. His partner, attired a bit less conservatively in university umber, didn't even look up. Lydia looked from one to the other, dipped the middle fingers of both hands simultaneously in her coffee, and flicked tiny liquid bombs like an ambidextrous gunfighter directly in their faces. They jerked to startled attention.

"Good afternoon," she repeated, smiling pleasantly.

"O, hi!" Brown said. "Sorry."

"Hello," muttered Umber. "Sorry. We got a bit involved there."

"You're forgiven. Since my husband left I find it easy to forgive cute young men." Brown and Umber looked at each other. They weren't quite sure how to take this. "Don't feel sorry for me, boys. He left me rich." And she smiled again. "Not only that," she added, "he left me permanently." Now they were smiling too.

"That oughta be worth half a board," Alan whispered to me.

If the first board were any indication, it was. I was seated between Alan and Umber, with only the colours vulnerable. Lydia was in first seat, taking her time, waiting for the normal round one hubbub to subside. Satisfied, she opened with a pass and Brownie followed with one diamond. This was the hand:

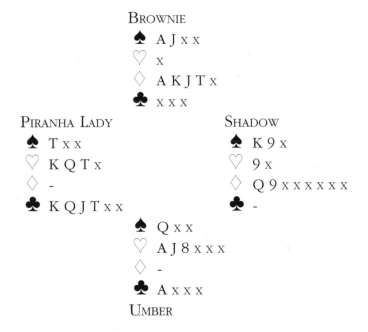

BROWNIE
♠ A J x x
♡ x
♢ A K J T x
♣ x x x

PIRANHA LADY
♠ T x x
♡ K Q T x
♢ -
♣ K Q J T x x

SHADOW
♠ K 9 x
♡ 9 x
♢ Q 9 x x x x x
♣ -

♠ Q x x
♡ A J 8 x x x
♢ -
♣ A x x x
UMBER

Brownie's opening had effectively erased any thoughts Alan might have had of introducing the suit. He passed, Umber bid one heart, and Lydia came to life with a three club call.

In those days, to be fair, double was not quite as 'automatic' as it would be in later years, and Brownie thought he might have a shot at the vulnerable three no trumps if he emphasised his diamonds and Umber had the right hand. Innocently he called three diamonds. Alan came out of the shadows with a double and Umber ran to his heart suit, hoping for a better landing place. The Piranha Lady, however, had just finished sharpening her teeth. Five hundred and all the matchpoints to the good guys.

"I was just doing the disciplined thing, like (censored) told me," she said later. "I couldn't open one club because I didn't have enough defensive tricks, and three clubs was bad because of the void and the possibility it might play better in hearts." She chuckled. "And it did; *their* hearts!"

A few more rounds brought to the table two of the contenders for that year's McKenny race, the precursor of the Barry Crane run for most masterpoints of the annum. The pros passed a grunt of recognition to Alan as they seated themselves, but fatally failed to accord proper respect to the Piranha Lady, who glared briefly at both of them over her reading glasses before pulling her cards from the board.

This was the first hand:

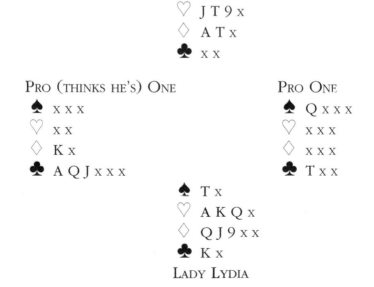

ALAN
- ♠ A K J x
- ♡ J T 9 x
- ◇ A T x
- ♣ x x

PRO (THINKS HE'S) ONE
- ♠ x x x
- ♡ x x
- ◇ K x
- ♣ A Q J x x x

PRO ONE
- ♠ Q x x x
- ♡ x x x
- ◇ x x x
- ♣ T x x

- ♠ T x
- ♡ A K Q x
- ◇ Q J 9 x x
- ♣ K x

LADY LYDIA

Lydia started with one diamond in first at unfavourable, and P.(t.h.)O. bid a confident two clubs. Alan doubled and Lydia rapped the table with a knuckle. P.O. grunted a pass. Lydia thought about it, and rejected any no trump calls for a jump to three hearts. After a pass Alan jumped to five hearts! Lydia folded her cards, put an elbow on her upmost knee, and plopped her chin into her palm.

Not a bid I would make playing with most people, but Alan certainly knew his customer. Later Lydia said she really wasn't certain whether Alan was looking for good trumps or just a club control, the other suits having been bid either directly or inferentially, but it didn't matter, since she had both. She bid a confident six hearts.

Pro (thinks he's) One wasn't about to lead his ace against an L.O.L., not even at pairs. He led the deuce of spades.

Not tempted to take the practice finesse, Lydia won both the spade ace and king, ruffed a spade with an honour, played a small trump to the nine, and ruffed the last spade with an honour as P.(t.h.) O. dumped a club. She cashed her remaining honour and led the queen of diamonds. When it was covered she won the ace, played the jack and ten of trumps, throwing her clubs, and showed her diamonds although P.O. was already jamming his hand back into the board with disgusting gusto.

"I've had bigger eggs," he muttered, "but I can't remember when!"

"Very well played, Lydia," Alan said, "*and* well bid!"

The big boys were so taken aback they let the next hand get stolen without punishment, and they left the table with an average minus to accompany the zero.

"O boys," Lydia called as they stood and began heading for the next table. She picked the scoreslip out of Alan's hand and flapped it at them. "Don't forget to sign the card..."

The next opponents were an attractive young local couple who introduced themselves as Linda and Laurence to Alan and greeted Lydia, whom they knew well, with genuine pleasure. They even welcomed me to their fair twin cities.

"Which would be even more fair if they held this damn tournament a month later," Lydia cut in.

"Minnesota's theatre of seasons," Linda quipped. "One act of mosquitoes between two acts of snow!"

The first hand saw the Shadow do a little defensive dancing.

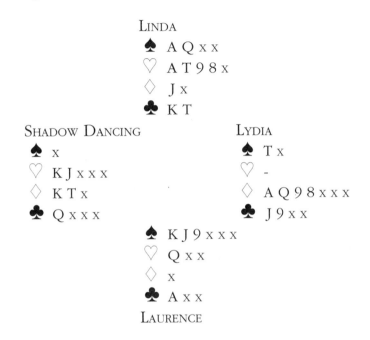

LINDA
♠ A Q x x
♡ A T 9 8 x
♢ J x
♣ K T

SHADOW DANCING
♠ x
♡ K J x x x
♢ K T x
♣ Q x x x

LYDIA
♠ T x
♡ -
♢ A Q 9 8 x x x
♣ J 9 x x

♠ K J 9 x x x
♡ Q x x
♢ x
♣ A x x
LAURENCE

Alan was dealer with nobody vulnerable, and started with a pass. Linda opened an Irish two diamonds (the Flannery convention), and Lydia bid *four* diamonds. Over Laurence's game bid in spades Alan had no problem taking the dive, and bid five diamonds. That rolled around to Laurence who bid one more spade for the road.

Alan led a thoughtful king of diamonds. Lydia placed the queen under it and Alan switched to the king of hearts. Lydia ruffed out the ace and there was still no way for Laurence to avoid an eventual heart loser.

"Nice play, Lydia," Alan said. "That was a thoughtful queen of diamonds."

Lydia turned to Laurence and placed a hand over his. " I hate to do it to such a cute young fellow, Laurence. Why don't you ditch Linda after the game and I'll make it up to you?"

"Hand us a top on this one and you can have him," Linda grinned, and pulled her next hand out.

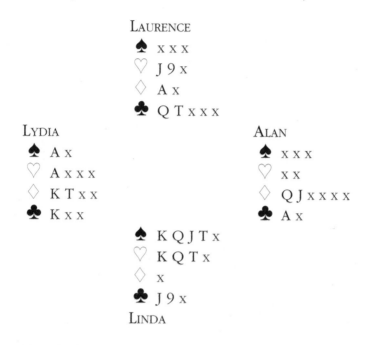

LAURENCE
♠ x x x
♡ J 9 x
♢ A x
♣ Q T x x x

LYDIA
♠ A x
♡ A x x x
♢ K T x x
♣ K x x

ALAN
♠ x x x
♡ x x
♢ Q J x x x x
♣ A x

♠ K Q J T x
♡ K Q T x
♢ x
♣ J 9 x
LINDA

With only their opponents vulnerable Linda started with one spade, Lydia doubled, Laurence bid two spades, and Alan three diamonds. Linda continued on to three spades, which got passed around to Alan.

"Do you have an understanding about three spades?" he asked Laurence. "A game try? Or competitive?"

"Not a try. Kinda like 1-2-3 Stop."

"You're not to bid no matter if you're at the top of your range?"

"Yeah; like that."

"Like double," Alan said.

Lydia led a little old ladylike fourth best, the deuce of hearts, which in this case turned out to be absolutely first best. Alan played his highest heart as the nine won in dummy. A spade went to the king and ace and the heart ace came right after it. When Alan followed with a baby heart Lydia turned to Linda.

"You mean what you said about loaning me Laurence after

the game if we hand you a top?" Her left eye said 'I'm kidding' and her right said 'I'm dead serious'.

"I'd better not, Lydia. There'd be nothing left for me."

"Damn. That's too bad." She gave Alan the heart ruff, and two clubs and a club ruff soon followed. Plus three hundred, slightly better than the one thirty available in diamonds.

Linda looked up at her husband and pouted, then signed the scoreslip Lydia had snatched from Alan to place gently before her.

"Well, she gave you a choice, love," Laurence chided as they left the table. "Personally I think you're underestimating my staying power."

Throughout the first session things continued to go well. Lydia seemed to pick the right time to do the right things against the right opponents. Those she missed taking a snap out of somehow managed to fall over dead anyway, and by the dinner break Lydia and Alan had won their section and were in the top three in the field.

"For the most part," Alan said over dinner, "I was helpless. I just bid my cards and followed suit. Most of the decisions were Lydia's and she was doing a fine job without me getting involved. Sometimes sitting back and minding your own business is the right thing to do."

"Are you going to kibitz the evening session, too?" Lydia asked me.

"Just a couple of rounds. My friend Patrick's coming by to take me on a memory tour of West Bank."

"Well, I think you should be watching me instead of (censored). He can be pretty dull sometimes."

Having already decided to do just that, I didn't tell Lydia it was so I could spot Patrick when he entered the playing area to fetch me. Now that she's playing bridge with the great Sky Shuffler I can let it out, but at the time I simply told her that it was already clear to me her entertainment value far exceeded Alan's, and I would consider it an honour to kibitz at her side. I don't suppose she bought all that, but she did give my cheek a healthy pinch. No, I'm *not* saying which cheek. Well, okay; the left one. Now you know she was right-handed.

The first round of the final session brought Lydia and Alan

to the table of the sweetest old couple they would ever have the misfortune to meet. That's where the wheels jumped the track.

I pulled up a seat beside Lydia just as the sweet little old man was passing a warning to his sweet little old lady.

"Remember, Millie, ven I bid four no trumpf is always how many aces haff you got. And if I fall asleep is because you vanted me to play second session, not because of schnapps, hokay?"

"Harold," Lydia admonished, "you didn't really have schnapps with dinner, did you? At your age?"

"Lydia, I haff schnapps *for* dinner. Millie tvist my arm to play two sessions so we make a deal."

"Deal is he keep his mouth shut too," Millie said.

"I keep it," said Harold, a crooked grin on his face.

On the first hand Lydia picked up, in fourth hand at favourable vulnerability: ♠T9 ♡xx ◇Qxxxxx ♣xxx. Harold passed and Alan started with one heart. Millie came in with two clubs, Lydia passed, and Harold raised to three clubs. A double by Alan fetched three diamonds from Lydia and four clubs from Harold. When Alan pushed on to four diamonds Sweet Little Old Lady Mildred put the boots to it. This was the whole hand:

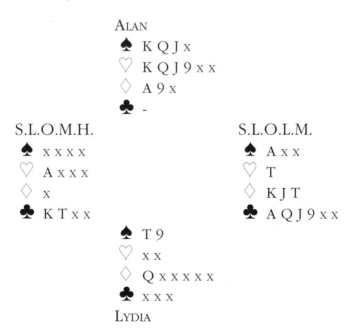

ALAN
♠ K Q J x
♡ K Q J 9 x x
◇ A 9 x
♣ -

S.L.O.M.H.
♠ x x x x
♡ A x x x
◇ x
♣ K T x x

S.L.O.L.M.
♠ A x x
♡ T
◇ K J T
♣ A Q J 9 x x

♠ T 9
♡ x x
◇ Q x x x x x
♣ x x x
LYDIA

Harold led a club, and every time the defense got in they led more clubs. With dummy trumpless Lydia led winning spades trying to induce Millie to ruff, thereby enabling one overruff to hold the loss to minus one hundred and a good score into the one thirty available in clubs the other way. But Millie blithely threw clubs and Lydia was forced to ruff and lead trumps from her hand. Minus three hundred and a near egg.

"Nice defense, Millie," Alan complemented.

"Vy you no trumpf that spade?" Harold demanded. "Ve beat it another."

"Vy you not keep your mouth shut like you promise?" Millie sweetly reminded. "Then you not haff to pull your foot out."

On the next hand the vulnerability was switched, Alan passed, and Mildred opened one spade holding:

♠AJxxx ♡AQx ◇xx ♣Qxx. That got a pass from Lydia and a quick 'Four No Trumpf!' from Harold. A moment later he bid a grand in no trump, disdaining a king check for the simple reason that he held them all: ♠Kx ♡KTxx ◇AKxx ♣AKx. That he was lacking a source of tricks bothered him not a whit. He won the opening lead of the queen of diamonds from Alan, cashed the king of spades and led a spade to the jack. Only for sweet little old men and ladies do the key suits break three-three with the queen in the lock. Alan chalked a stoic zero on his scorecard.

"You're a lucky kibitzer, young man," Millie told me. "Sure you von't stay around?"

"I don't think you need any help," I smiled, and dragged my seat to the next table. There waited a pair of middle-aged local sharks who were busy complementing themselves as Alan and Lydia took their places.

"Don't break your wrists on each other's back, boys," Lydia said, and proceeded to break their backs.

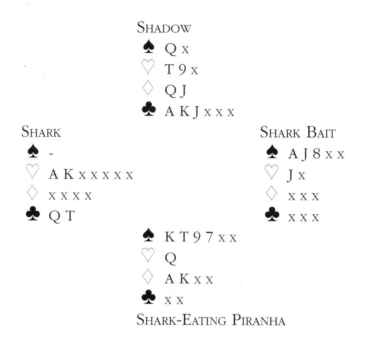

Shadow
♠ Q x
♡ T 9 x
♢ Q J
♣ A K J x x x

Shark
♠ -
♡ A K x x x x x
♢ x x x x
♣ Q T

Shark Bait
♠ A J 8 x x
♡ J x
♢ x x x
♣ x x x

♠ K T 9 7 x x
♡ Q
♢ A K x x
♣ x x

Shark-Eating Piranha

The Shark dealt at favourable and started with four hearts, passed around to the Piranha who fearlessly balanced with four spades. That went around to Shark Bait, who thought it would play better in eight spades. When it got back to the Shadow he bumped the ante to sixteen spades, just to show his confidence in his partner.

The Shark started a top heart and continued a middle one after a brief look at dummy. Lydia ruffed and led a trump, playing the queen when the Shark showed out. Shark Bait, with a trifle too much impatience icing his greed, won the ace and switched to a diamond. Lydia ducked to the dummy, led a spade and finessed cheaply, and led a club up. When the ace-king set up the suit she simply pounded winners through Bait, tossing the ace of diamonds along the way for a little flair.

"Swell," said the Shark. "One of my better preempts at these colours, too." Shark Bait wilted.

Then the Piranha Lady, perhaps tiring of nibbling pieces off opponents, sunk her teeth into the Shadow's ankle and dragged him kicking and screaming into the stratospheric level of an anti-percentage slam.

LYDIA
♠ A K
♡ K x
♢ A K 9 8
♣ A 9 8 7 x

♠ J T x x
♡ A Q x x
♢ x x
♣ J T x

SHAKY SHADOW

Starting with one club in third, Lydia reversed into diamonds over Alan's one heart response. Perhaps a two no trump call at this point would have been best, but Alan usually likes to support partner at the earliest opportunity. In character, he preferred to three clubs, which certainly promised no extras but for some reason gave Lydia a rosy perspective of her own first bid suit. She forced with three spades and Alan naturally called the no trump game. The next peep from Lydia was a direct jump to the no trump slam!

Bait led the queen of diamonds.

"Robust reverse, partner," Alan said. "Thank you very much."

Prospects were about as bright as a firefly in a mudbath. Entries appeared to be the least of Alan's problems. As he studied the hand I saw Patrick enter the room. I stood briefly and caught his attention with a wave. I flashed him two fingers.

"I have to get going," I said quietly to Lydia. She clamped a hand on my thigh.

"Maybe you'd like to have a game with me later in the week?"

"It would be a pleasure," I said. "I'll talk to you tomorrow."

I stood and patted the Shadow's shoulder as I walked by. "Sorry to interrupt. Gotta go."

"Call me after the session." He went back to his study, and I headed for the door where Patrick was waiting.

"Let's go to Caesar's," Patrick said as we stepped outside. "There's a pair of identical twins I want you to meet."

"Attractive?"

"*Beyond* beauty. Their mother's a twin, and she had seven births, all of *them* twins except for one, and he's the bartender."

"Not too protective, I hope."

"Very. And into karate."

"Great." The sarcasm dripped like drool from the lips of a baby.

*　*　*

I need not have feared. Brothers are putty in the hands of an infatuated sister.

Late into a wonderful evening I slipped to the pay phone and rang the Shadow's room at the hotel.

"Mikey! Glad you called. I've just been sitting around getting blasted in lonely celebration. Why don't you drop over?"

"Celebration? You won?!?"

"Indeed we did. Lydia's second regional title, first pairs. That six no you left on was the hand that did it."

"What happened?"

"You remember the hand?"

"I remember Lydia's; and the auction."

He filled me in with his hand. "At trick two I led a low club from the dummy, my jack won by the king on my left. Another diamond left me in the dummy again. The ace of clubs dropped the queen on my right! Some days you've gotta be lucky. The east-west cards were:

HUMBLED SHARK BAIT	SHARK CHAGRINED
♠ x x x	♠ Q x x x
♡ x x x	♡ J T x x
♢ Q J T x	♢ x x x
♣ K x x	♣ Q x

Can you work out what I did now?"

"No prob. Cashed the ace-king of spades and the puppy tracks and pinched the ugly one in the majors. A 'double' Vienna coup!"

"Bingo. So you comin' over?"

"No, I ran into something that puts bridge and you both in the back seat."

"Red?"

"Brunette."

"Later." The phone went dead. I headed back into Caesar's.

Shadow on Frozen Tundra

THE PLANE WAS ON ITS GLIDE PATH, descending into Edmonton. We still had to be over a hundred kilometres out and five high when RJ, my friend and sometime business cohort, leaned across me and peered out the window. There's not much to see when it's forty-two below zero on the ground. A lot of white, and an infinite number of infinitesimal ice particles dancing with light in the air.

"Gawd," RJ drawled with humour dry as a mouthful of talcum, "I can see the mukluks already."

Normally one does not look forward to flying into Edmonton on a February morning. There is cold, and there is *cold*. And *then* there's Edmonton. But in addition to the business that brought me was the anticipation of a prearranged (He couldn't sneak up on me *this* time!) meeting with the Shadow.

Alan was in Edmonton to curl in a big money bonspiel, throwing second rock for one of the best known names in the sport. We were to meet at La Boheme, my single favourite dwelling place in town, where he had most of the afternoon and evening free and where we could catch up with each other over a meal unparalleled in the prairie provinces.

La Boheme is a refurbished turn-of-the-century three-storey apartment block in northeast Edmonton. The top two floors are devoted to one and two-bedroom suites, the kind with high ceilings and wooden floors and deep and comfortable clawfoot tubs in the bathroom. The furnishings are French Provincial, the ambience continental, and the food and service impeccable. The main floor houses the famed restaurant, a lounge decorated with a wall of harlequins, and a pattisserie where fresh baked croissants are prepared for morning delivery to the room with strong coffee and sweet orange juice. In the basement is a wine cellar of the first order and a tasting room for the connoisseur.

I met the Shadow shortly after three in the lounge. Although I was unfamiliar with his curling persona, it wasn't hard to pick him out. Since he couldn't be one of the two well-attired young women in above-the-knee wool suits (only in Edmonton, when the Fahrenheit temperature is equal to the centigrade), he had to be the only other person there, a portly fellow wearing brown horn-rimmed glasses and a navy-blue cap.

"It has to be you," I said as I approached.

"Who else would I be but me?" a familiar voice answered.

"You put on some weight since I last saw you," I chided as I sat down.

"Yeah, but two pounds of latex doesn't move around a whole heck of a lot different than twenty pounds of blubber. Helps my delivery, 'though. Improves my balance in the slide tucking my thigh into this rounded gut."

"Or perhaps more accurately wrapping your rounded gut around your thigh. Nice look. Weren't you my home room teacher in grade five?"

"I was everybody's. That's what happens when you look like Everyman. Can I buy you a drink?"

I'd been waiting for that. I caught the eye of the barmaid. "Double Hennessey XO, please," I said. "Side of cappuccino....make it two," I added, catching Alan nod at me.

"It's nice to get some time off from the curling. I'm looking forward to dinner after all your raving about the food."

"You won't be disappointed."

"How about afterward? Think we can find some bridge?"

"What, you getting tired of throwing a forty-two pound rock down a hundred and twenty odd feet of ice and trying to stop it on a dime?"

"Desperately."

"Well, sorry to disappoint. Actually, another friend I want you to meet is coming by later. He's in the computer science department at the university. Thought we'd socialise and maybe get into some music."

"Fine with me."

"Just one thing...I don't know your damn name."

He laughed. "Call me Rob."

* * *

Bridge is unusual in many ways. One of these is that you don't always have to go looking for it. Sometimes it finds you.

Alan and I were lingering over cognacs after a typically exquisite La Boheme feast when we were joined by my friend Colin and another mutual friend, Mark, whom Colin had dragged away from his computer terminal. Over introductions and another cognac it was decided we would go to Colin's favourite campus hangout, a pub populated by an eclectic mixture of staff, graduate students, and undergrads, where we could partake of the traditional triumvirate of wine, women, and song.

Other than fingernails on blackboards the sound I hate worst is that of snow squeaking underfoot. The squeak becomes harsher as the temperature lowers. Colin parked more than a block from the pub, and we all had a chilly trudge on the frozen tundra, with the steps from eight bustling feet pressing into the packed snow and throwing up a cacophony of squeaks that tapdanced up my spine and nipped at every nerve ending from my tailbone to my ears. We shouldered into the pub to find ourselves standing in a mob of undergrads. We had to raise our voices over the hubbub.

"We may have made a small error," Colin admitted. The beer crowd was out in full force. No staff or grads here, where a quieter mode of conversation with perhaps more substance than the sexual proclivities of a rock singer might be found. Wine was beer, women were girls, and song was rap, the only thing worse than disco. "Friday wasn't a good choice of nights."

"We're here now,"Mark said. "I'll find us a table somewhere."

"There's no way I'm going back outside," I said. "I don't suppose there's a potbellied stove around here I can sit on for a while...?"

"I'm going to check the place out," Alan put a hand on my shoulder. "I'll be at the back. Looks like it might be quieter there."

Mark had timely luck, nabbing a table in a far front corner, right next to the window, just as another group vacated it. I was about to sit down when I saw Alan above the crowd near the back, motioning to me to join him. When I had fought through the bodies and neared him he pointed over his shoulder. I followed the line of his finger.

A small anteroom held a half dozen tables of chatting students. More accurately, it held five. The sixth was a group of four young males, each with thirteen cards in his hands.

"Can you believe it?" Alan said. "Ask and ye shall receive. This could be interesting." I nodded and we edged closer until we were leaning against the wall in prime kibitzer territory.

It was soon apparent there was a rank beginner among the novices.

A young man with long blond hair and a wispy blond goatee peered through granny glasses at the thirteen cards he used two hands to hold. His brows were lit in puzzlement, his face pink with self-consciousness. He held five-five in the reds and didn't know what to do next as all three showered him with advice that would have been meaningless even had it been relevant. To add to the young fellow's discomfiture he was burdened with a harelip and a massive speech impediment. He was not the picture of a happy camper.

The Shadow took pity.

"Hi guys," he broke in. "What's the game?"

Blondey's LHO looked over his shoulder and glared at Alan, taking in the pot belly and middle America duds. He was obviously the table expert, a three-quarter size fellow about twenty with good looks, Clark Kent hair so black it had blue highlights, and self-assurance in enough abundance to parcel out freely to those with less, and not notice any missing.

"Bridge, donkey-orifice," he said contemptuously, glancing briefly at me to let me into his perceived group of ignorance. "Get lost." And he turned back to the table. The other two young men seemed embarrassed, but said nothing. Blondey's partner, a lanky lad wearing a black tee shirt and backwards baseball cap, lit himself a cigarette. Blondey's RHO, moonfaced under a mop of dark hair like steel wool, began inspecting the bottom of his beer glass.

Alan appeared to ignore the comment directed at us. Instead he walked behind Blondey and leaned over his shoulder, peering into his hand, which was: ♠xxx ♡QJ9xx ♢AJ9xx ♣-, and saying, "What's the bidding been up to now?"

Suddenly three sets of eyes were glancing quickly at each other. After a few false starts the bidding was revealed to have gone, on this first hand of the rubber:

BLACK CAPBACK	MOONFACE	BLONDEY	CLARKEY K.
P	1 ♠	P	2 ♣
2 ♡	3 ♠	?	

This was where Blondey's problem came in. Should he bid hearts, or perhaps diamonds, since they were better and partner had already mentioned hearts? The Shadow whispered in his ear.

"You and your partner are a team; you're two halves of the same coin. Your first duty should be to show him your support."

"Phorts!" said Blondey. Clarkey K. bid four spades and it came back to Blondey. He looked over his shoulder at his Shadow, an imploring whipped Bassett Hound kind of look. "Now what?" he said.

"Now we think about the bidding we heard and try to form a picture of the distribution of the hands in our minds. Like this. First your guy on the right here has bid spades and rebid them while jumping the bidding. How many spades you think he has?"

"Lots."

"How lots?"

"Thix, maybe."

"Good. And the mouth on your left has supported spades, so he should have a few. Add in yours and how many do you think your partner is looking at?"

Blondey's eyes lit up. "None!"

"Good again. None, maybe one. So if you guys play hearts how many black suit tricks you think you'll lose?"

"The thame!"

"Great. Let's go on. How many hearts has partner?"

"Phive or thix?"

"To the what?"

"Aith or king."

"How about clubs?"

"*He* bid them." He jerked a thumb at Clarkey.

"Sure, so he's got five or six, his partner a few, and *your* partner?"

"I get it! Phorer phive. Tho he'th only got one or two diamondth!"

"Kid, I think you can be a player. Now think about the two hands pieced together. Count potential losers."

"No clubth, none or one diamond, a heart, none or one thpade. One to three lootherth!"

"And neither one of you has an opening hand. What do you think you should do now?"

"Bid phive hearth!"

"So what are you waiting for? This game is taking long enough."

"Five hearth!" said Blondey. Two passes were greeted by a resounding double from Moonface, who led out two rounds of spades. Backcap's hand was: ♠x ♡ATxxxx ◇QT ♣xxxx. Hearts were 1-1, the king of diamonds was in the lock, and not even Backcap could fail to make an overtrick.

Blondey was delighted. He jumped up from his chair and grabbed Alan's elbow with two hands, pulling him into it, insisting Alan play because they'd only roped Blondey in as a desperation fourth when the lady from the law department was tardy making her appearance. Alan would only have to play until she showed, and Blondey would much rather watch, as long as Alan explained things to him as they went along. Little did Blondey know he had spoken, or at least uttered, the magic words. There was little likelihood Alan would have refused a chance to put Blondey's torturers in a humble bubble at any rate, but an opportunity to play Terence Reese to a captive audience over his shoulder was simply too good to resist.

With no further persuasion the Shadow settled into his seat and picked up, now vulnerable in second position, the type of hand I get when I *dream* of rubber bridge:

♠- ♡AKJTx ♢AKT9xx ♣A.

After a pass by Moonface Alan opened two diamonds. Clarkey came in with three clubs and Backcap with three spades. Alan leaned around to Blondey and whispered, "I could bid four hearts now, but I might play there. If I cuebid my lefty's club suit, which shows a first round control and a great hand, maybe my partner can show me some diamond support."

Except over the four club cue Backcap bid four hearts! "Even better," Alan said to Blondey. "Let's do it again. Tell me how many diamonds are in my partner's hand." Blondey thought about it.

"I'm not thure," he said.

"He's bid two suits; what's the minimum cards he has in both togcther?"

"Nine."

"Minimum. Did he support diamonds?"

"No. Two or leth."

"Good. Now presuming he didn't bid hearts on four little and that he has the queen, how many losers do you see when you paste the two hands together?"

After a moment or two another bright light turned on in Blondey's brain. "None!"

"Your bid," Alan offered.

"Theven hearth!" Blondey squealed in delight. Backcap had another suitable hand, although it was hard to imagine any that could be unsuitable: ♠Axxxxx ♡Qxxx ◇J ♣xx. Alan pointed out how the spade ace was wasted and how even the right yarborough might produce a grand. Blondey was nodding with understanding, his eyes alive with interest. It was like watching a brain wired to a rheostat brighten as the gain was slowly turned up.

That had been one rubber over quickly. Alan dealt the first hand of the next, shuffling and dealing the cards with the flying fingers of a Vegas pro. Glances bounced around the table like pinballs as he dealt; it was becoming rapidly apparent a hawk had landed amongst the sparrows. Moreover, there was a subtle psychological phenomenon occurring. The Shadow was *Blondey's* hawk. Blondey was sitting tall and straight in his chair, which had it been any closer to Alan's would have been been grafting itself. The flush had faded from his face. In its place was deep interest and heady anticipation. He was no longer the table whipping boy. He was the circus lion tamer, and the Shadow was his whip.

This was the next hand:

BACKCAP
♠ J x x x
♡ A x x x
◇ A J x
♣ K J

CLARKEY K.
♠ A Q T 9 x
♡ K J 9
◇ 9
♣ 9 x x x

MOONFACE
♠ x x
♡ T x x x
◇ Q x x x
♣ x x x

♠ K x
♡ Q x
◇ K T 8 x x
♣ A Q T x
SHADOW

CLARKEY K.	BACKCAP	MOONFACE	SHADOW
P	1 ♣(!)	P	1 ◇
1 ♠	DBL(!)	P	3NT
P	P	P	

Backcap demonstrated his virtuosity with the 'short club' and ensuing rebids and the Shadow soon found himself in the notrump game on Clarkey K.'s lead of fourth best from his longest and strongest. Alan won the king and led a diamond up, noting the Scottish curse rise on his left. He won the ace and pounded the jack through Moonface, and on the run of the minors Superboy got squeezed in the majors, having to strip down to the stiff spade ace and king-jack tight of hearts. At trick eleven Alan explained to Blondey the three cards Clarkey K. was down to, and invited Blondey to make the play. Blondey smiled and extracted the baby spade from Alan's hand. Three overtricks brought a concerned burp from Backcap.

"Should I have raised three no?" he asked.

"I don't think so."

"Ith there a name phor that?" Blondey wondered aloud.

"You bet," Alan said. "It's called a strip squeeze and endplay. On the run of my winners he was squeezed out of his and forced to strip to an ending, in this case one of three cards, where he was uncomfortable. Then he was thrown in with his spade to be endplayed into leading away from his king of hearts."

"I think I thee it. I thee the ending anyway!" Blondey said excitedly.

"If you do, you're way ahead of half the bridge world," Alan answered. The kid glowed.

Vulnerable again, Backcap and the Shadow returned to the breech.

BACKCAP
♠ A
♡ Q T 9 x
♢ A 9 x x x x
♣ A Q

♠ x x x
♡ A K J x
♢ J T x x
♣ x x
SHADOW

BACKCAP	MOONFACE	SHADOW	CLARKEY K.
1 ♢	2 ♣	3 ♢	P
3 ♡	3 ♠	4 ♡	P
P	P		

It wasn't hard to see Alan was wishing negative doubles were a part of the pub repertoire, but since he had a one bid hand at the three level he contented himself with supporting his partner as his first obligation. Along with setting a good example, of course. He even got to set it twice, as Backcap trotted out the heart suit for the third time in four hands.

Moonface led a baby diamond, clearly singleton, and Backcap topped Clarkey's (falsecarded) king with the ace. He drew trumps in three rounds ending in dummy and took the practice finesse in clubs. Making only one overtrick. But winning another fast rubber.

Alan quickly scribbled the hand down on the back of a cardboard beer coaster and showed it to Blondey while Moonface was dealing the next one. The club queen was now a deuce.

"Pretend you're in a slam," Alan said, "and there's no queen of clubs to take a finesse with for your twelfth trick. Pretend also you're playing the hand from my side. You have to lose a diamond, but that leaves five diamond winners. The two black aces make seven, and four trumps makes eleven. What would *you* do for an extra trick?"

"Trump a thpade in the dummy?" Blondey wondered.

"Bingo! Even though it was played from your buddy's side, all he had to do was exactly that - trump a spade loser in his hand. In effect he gets five trump winners instead of four. He has to be careful about knocking out the big diamond before trumping the spade, or else there's no trumps left in the dummy and when they get in with the diamond they'll be able to cash a spade before you can throw your last one on the long diamond...Do you understand?"

"I'm not really thure."

Alan looked at him. "Then you're another step up on other players. Most of them have too much damn ego to ever admit they don't understand. You've got the right attitude, kid. You'll learn, and you'll do it faster than most." This time Blondey almost blushed. "That last play is called a dummy reversal, when you trump losers in your hand instead of in the dummy. In your mind you sort of step around the table and play it from your partner's side. Since he *did* own the queen of clubs slam is always cold from his side, because a club lead through the ace-queen may beat the hand when it's played from my side. You just don't have time to get rid of the club loser and you would be forced to take the finesse at trick one. The thing is, there's a way to bid it from his side, but it all comes down to walking before you run. One day you'll know how to sprint."

By then Moonface had the cards dealt:

BACKCAP
♠ A 9 x x
♡ K J T x
◊ Q T
♣ 9 8 7

♠ Q T
♡ x
◊ A K J 9 8 x
♣ Q J x x
SHADOW

MOONFACE	SHADOW	CLARKEY K.	BACKCAP
P	1 ◊	1 ♡	1 ♠
DBL	2 ♣	P	2NT
P	3NT	P	P
P			

Moonface led his partner's bid suit and on this hand Blondey got to learn about all kinds of finesses - indirect ones, as in spades, where the king was marked on the bidding, and finesses against spots, such as the club ten, which was happily in the lock, and finesses when the opponents lead something you're out of, such as the heart ten or jack when Clarkey fired the suit back. Nine tricks came home and the Shadow was vulnerable again.

To no one's surprise by now, and certainly not his, he once again held a fistful of girl's best friends:

BACKCAP
♠ Q J x x x
♡ x x
◇ 8 7 x
♣ K x x

♠ A
♡ A J x
◇ A K T 9 x x
♣ J T x
SHADOW

The auction was simple but not especially sweet. Alan opened one diamond and rebid three diamonds over Backcap's one spade. The auction should naturally have ended there, but Backcap thought his spades worth another call. When Alan bid three notrump Clarkey, holding queen-jack fourth of diamonds and assorted other cards, put some well-judged boots to it. Alan soon conceded one down and congratulated Clarkey on his double.

It was then everyone noticed the regular fourth, the lady from the law school, had made her appearance, and just in time to see Alan go one down doubled.

Alan relinquished his seat willingly, and held it for the young woman as she took his place. Then he hunkered down beside Blondey.

"If you're serious about learning, pick up Audrey Grant's stuff and take it from there, or check out the local bridge club, where they probably teach from her series. Take all the drivel you hear around this place about short clubs or anything else and let it go in one ear and out the other. Learn the basics from her stuff and find a partner who will learn it with you, because above all, this is a partnership game. And good luck. I think you'll be all right."

Blondey stuck out his hand. His eyes were brimming with nothing short of moist idolatry. Not only had this knowledgeable stranger rescued him from his embarrassment, he had treated him with dignity, accorded his intelligence, and praised his attitude to boot.

"Thankth a lot, mithter," he said. "Really. Thank you," he emphasised in his handshake.

"I'd be lying if I didn't say it was really *my* pleasure, kid. See you around, sometime, somewhere."

He stood up. "So long, guys. Thanks for the game."

"You had your luck," Clarkey K. said.

"I don't deny it," Alan answered. "But you gotta hold them before you can dance with them. Later."

As we turned into the crowd Lady Law piped up, "Who was *that?*"

"He never said," Backcap answered. "But he's some helluva player."

"Not from what *I* saw," she sniffed.

Shadow on the Rails

RIDING THE RAILS IS ONE OF THE BEST ways I know of imbuing the psyche with a sense of peace and contentment. Would that the idiot powers-that-be who run the Canadian railroad understood that fact.

What can be finer than the harmonious marriage of motion, sound, and sight, blended together like sun-warmed acrylics on an artist's palette, transferred to the mind as if brushed on a canvas? Where else can the anxieties of the day be shelved by the sense of being carried down the fallopian tube of life, being gently jostled from side to side in a stream of passing scenery while the mind, lulled by the steady and muted staccato of wheel on rail, mulls on times past and times to come?

Of course, the Canadian government, ipso facto mismanager of Via Rail, doesn't see it that way. Dimwitted and determined, it attempts simply to lose as little money as possible, cutting services instead of implementing them, ignoring client convenience and comforts rather than catering to them. In the continuing quest to alienate the customer trunk lines have been abandoned, food has been institutionalised, schedules have been cut. Why learn from Japanese or European when it's so much easier to copy American?

The Shadow had suggested I turn in my plane ticket and join him on the train through the Rockies from frigid Edmonton to mild Vancouver. He didn't have to twist my arm, seeing as he had reserved for himself the finest private compartment offered. In this case that meant a roomette with two chairs, two thirty-six inch bunks, and a pissoir so small you had to unzip before you entered or get your elbows cracked on the walls. All this for only six hundred bucks one way.

The one compensation, other than the psyche-stroking, was the passage through the majesty of the Rocky Mountains. Of course Via Rail, in a marvellous display of timing and foresight, has seen fit to schedule departure from Edmonton in the morning, arriving in Jasper in mid-afternoon, and leaving just in time for the February sunsets. That this means passing through the entire mountain range in the black of night seems to have escaped their perception.

The Trip's the thing. If only the transit troglodytes could learn that. The train-travelling public doesn't give a damn what time the trains leave or arrive, only that they do so punctually. They'll happily climb aboard at four ayem in the middle of Anywhere, Nowhere if it means being able to spend the day passing through the glory of the mountains.

* * *

It was midnight, and I was staring through the window at pine-dotted mountainside and granite cliff. Unfortunately all I could see was my own disgusted reflection looking back at me. Alan had gone to the lounge an hour before, to read over brandy and coffee. At that time I'd been tired, but I soon found my mind too occupied to sleep, still thinking about the Shadow's adventure at the university pub. It would be nice, I thought, if someday the Bridge world had a star with golden blond hair, bad eyes, and a harelip.

I found the Shadow in the lounge, surrounded by a half dozen brandies, three cups of coffee, and two attractive ladies apparently on the sunny side of forty.

"Mikey!" Alan said, "We were just thinking of waking you up."

"I should think so," I answered, quickly surveying the scene. I'd forgotten another nice thing about train travel, namely the social aspect, the adventure of meeting new people.

Beth was a lanky brunette dressed in slacks and sweater, and exactly the same age as Jack Benny.

"For another twenty-two days," she said, freely admitting to her fortieth birthday around the proverbial corner. I would have believed a decade younger until I sat down and caught her eyes in the light. The crinkles at the edges and the directness with which she studied me *sans* self-consciousness told me the lady had seen enough of life through the veils and seams to know the difference between bull and brains. "That's why Dini and I are on this trip, to celebrate."

Dini was attractive but dour. She extended her hand as we were introduced and shook mine firmly with a single, quick pump. She wore a soft grey wool suit, complementing her jet black hair trimmed into a stylish and appealing pixie cut. Her voice was the gravel-ground timbre of the habitual smoker.

"Hi, heard you like to play bridge," were her first words, taking me by surprise.

"Alan's been revealing my private weaknesses, I see."

"Just the one," Beth smiled. "I tried to pry a few others out of him, but he'd hear nothing of it."

Well, well, I thought. The lady's *in*terested. The fledgling flight of innuendo has just left the nest. I looked at Alan. His palms were in the air as he shrugged at me.

"What are friends for?" he asked with panache and originality.

"We've been wanting to find a game since Thunder Bay," Dini said. "We were going to wake you up for a fourth."

"I must have heard the cards calling," I smiled.

"How about another round and we'll get started?" Alan offered. As we nodded, me perhaps most demonstratively, he raised his hand and called the waiter's attention. "Four of the same, please," he said. "Make one a double."

* * *

Shortly thereafter there we were, not where I'd first expected hopefully to be.

Beth won the cut, keeping up a pleasant patter as she dealt the cards.

"I hope you guys don't mind playing set," she said. "Dini and I just don't feel comfortable misbidding hands with other partners." She smiled at both of us, but with me she used her eyes as well as her lips.

"We're a team; we like to keep it that way." Dini said, glancing at me from under her eyebrows. Oops, I thought, innuendo number two has just taken flight. And from an entirely different nest.

I turned my attention to my cards, the better to enable me to mind my own damn business.

And I picked up: ♠T9xxx ♡T ◇AKxx ♣xxx.

Beth opened an Acol two hearts on my left, Alan passed, and Dini immediately jumped to a no trump game.

"Who cut these cards?" I quipped.

"You, pard," Alan said.

Beth now bid four diamonds, Dini four spades, and Beth six hearts, closing the auction with a flourish. Alan led the Curse of Ireland, and I cursed it.

DOUR DINI
♠ A J x x
♡ 9 x
◇ Q x x x
♣ K x x

SUFFERING SHADOW
♠ x x
♡ x x x x
◇ J x x
♣ 9 8 7 x

MALIGNED MIKEY
♠ T 9 x x x
♡ T
◇ A K x x
♣ J x x

♠ K Q
♡ A K Q J x x
◇ x x
♣ A Q T
BEDAZZLING BETH

"Nice bid!" Alan exclaimed. "It got me."

"It didn't get me," I smiled. "But unfortunately the bidding doesn't go counter-clockwise."

Beth giggled and patted my hand with a little 'there-there' gesture. Fortunately Dini was too busy writing up the score to notice.

"Those bids are three to one in favour of working," Beth said modestly. "There wasn't much to it. If there was a way of knowing she had jack and a fourth spade I would have bid seven." O. Very nice. Who were these ladies?

Then Alan dealt this little gem:

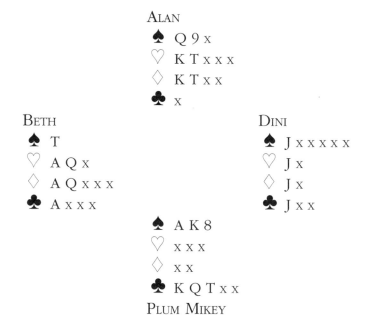

ALAN
♠ Q 9 x
♡ K T x x x
♢ K T x x
♣ x

BETH
♠ T
♡ A Q x
♢ A Q x x x
♣ A x x x

DINI
♠ J x x x x x
♡ J x
♢ J x
♣ J x x

♠ A K 8
♡ x x x
♢ x x
♣ K Q T x x

PLUM MIKEY

After two passes I opened one of my better major, a ploy I like when playing Drury, but normally at any other vulnerability and preferably with a stiff in my hand. Beth doubled, Alan raised me to two spades, and Dini doubled. After three passes I worked out responsive doubles were not part of their system.

Beth considered her lead, finally playing the club ace. She switched to her trump as soon as she saw the dummy.

I won in hand with the king, cashed two clubs, and led a

diamond up, hoping diamonds were 4-3 or 3-4 and that I could score my trumps separately. Beth played the *queen*. Now there was no way I could get off dummy without letting Dini in to come a trump. Although I scored the spade eight *en passant* I was still one in the toilet.

"Nice play," Alan and I said in unison to Beth.

"Thanks. If you'd led a heart I would have played the queen there, too."

"I have no doubt of it," I smiled. Who *were* these ladies?

Dour Dini dealt the third hand, unaware some kneesies were being tentatively toyed under the table. Suspicious sort that I am, I wondered if it were a small ploy intended to distract, but judging from twinkle in Beth's (I now took note) hazel eyes, I doubted it. Innuendo had already been shelved in favour of coquetry.

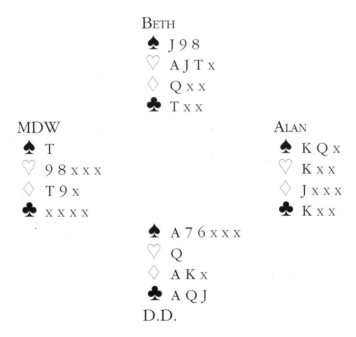

BETH
♠ J 9 8
♡ A J T x
♢ Q x x
♣ T x x

MDW
♠ T
♡ 9 8 x x x
♢ T 9 x
♣ x x x x

ALAN
♠ K Q x
♡ K x x
♢ J x x x
♣ K x x

♠ A 7 6 x x x
♡ Q
♢ A K x
♣ A Q J
D.D.

Dee Dee started with one spade, and Beth responded one no trump, disdaining the immediate spade raise with her pancake hand. Dini now rebid three diamonds(!), encouraging the possibility of a club lead, whatever the final contract. In her mind it was certain not to be no trump at any rate. Now Beth called three spades, Dini cued the club ace, and Beth the heart ace, and Dini hopped to Binsky in spades. Beth had had enough and passed. I tabled the nine of hearts.

Dini won the ace, and immediately played the jack of spades, floating it when Alan ducked. When my ten was smothered under it she smiled and took the club hook. When that worked she cashed the ace of spades and threw Alan in with another, tabling her hand.

"An overtrick," she said, "presuming you have both the rounded kings."

"Very well played!" Alan was no less thrilled when an opponent painted the canvas with an artist's touch as he was when he or his partner did.

"Yes, Dini," Beth said. "Well played."

"Ditto from me," I added.

That was one *quick* quick rubber. Butch, this is Sundance. Who the hell *are* these ladies?

* * *

We played a few more rubbers, the bridge going on till past three in the morning. The Shadow and I managed to hold our own the rest of the session, but it was more than apparent Beth and Dini knew what they were doing. They pushed us around in the auctions, and they played and defended well.

We had agreed that one pair would switch seats after each rubber, so that we could have our opponents on each side. It hardly mattered. Throughout the session first my left knee and thigh, then my right, was subjected to talented stroking of the first order.

Little of this was lost on Dini, who doubled me in a major game more on spite than good sense, on a hand where I had briefly considered making a slam try. I shipped it back and made exactly four.

"That was unnecessary, Dini," Beth said.

"Sorry, you're right," Dini answered, and in an immediate change of behaviour soon began yawning.

We decided to call it a night. The scenery outside hadn't changed a whit, and dawn in the mountains was still hours away.

Dini stood up, looked directly at me. "Goodnight," she said. Then she turned to Alan and said, "Thanks for the game." Beth hadn't moved. "G'night, Beth," Dini said last. "See you later."

"'Night," said Beth, picking up her coffee. Ain't body language grand?

Alan, quick to take a cue, looked at Dini's receding back and stood up.

"See you later," he said to us, and was gone like the Shadow he is.

Beth and I looked at each other and smiled.

"You and Dini have played before," I said, "but I've never seen you around the tournaments."

"We're from (censored). We've played in the European championships for our country."

I nodded. "Now I understand."

"What do you understand?" Beth asked, in the direct manner common to her country.

"I understand why you and Dini play so well together," I said, not entirely ignorant of innuendo or multiple entendre myself.

"We've been a... partnership for many years," she said. Then she leaned forward, instantly deducing and flirting with the very edge of my social distance. "...But I *do* like a man from time to time. Especially one with enough woman in him to be appealing."

"I'm not sure how to take that," I said, wondering as I spoke if I were lying.

"Take it like an offer." Well. That was direct enough to penetrate even the titanium that passes for my skull.

"O, well. Unlucky at cards..." I said. "Let's find a conductor. There's always an empty sleeper somewhere..."

Clickety clack, clickety clack.

Shadow in Reno

Ask any gambler. In Nevada it's easy to lose track of time. Ask any bridge player. It's even easier.

I arrived in Reno two days before the year-end regional, early on Christmas Eve, the better to acclimate myself to the surroundings. Acclimation in this case being to get friendly with a few blackjack dealers before the horde of bridge players inundated the tables on Boxing Day and reduced everyone playing for less than a hundred dollar minimum bet to faceless automatons donating chips to the house. Being early also affords me an opportunity to book ahead any popular shows for which it may be difficult to obtain tickets later. Like Mac Davis or Garth Brooks or New Year's Eve rides at the Mustang Ranch.

I checked into the Bally, had a fine pasta dinner, a short nap, and hit the tables somewhere near nine, keeping my bets small and chatting up the dealers while tipping them most of my earnings. It didn't take long to

find two of them who would be working late. I stuck to their
tables, taking frequent short breaks when they did, and a long
break after midnight to rest and recharge while the casino crowd
thinned. It's always best to play a dealer head to head, and
easiest to find one in the wee hours.

* * *

Time passed as I ground out the nickels and dimes.

I was up a hard-earned dollar and a half somewhere
between three and four in the morning when I began to tire, and
decided to call it a night. I was heading for the elevators when
struck with a case of Gambler's Tingle that shot from my coccyx
to my medulla oblongata.

There, standing alone behind the last table before the slots,
was one of the three most attractive natural redheads I have ever
seen in my life. Before her, seeming to my tired eyes to be
surrounded by an aura, was a single deck of cards. I didn't need
an engraved invitation to approach.

"Good morning," I said, letting my eyes smile at her.

"Good morning," she smiled back. Even my armpits were
tingling.

I indicated the deck with a quick glance. "You don't appear
to be the kind of lady that'd shuffle halfway through," I said.

"There's one way to find out," she answered, still smiling,
and offered me the One seat.

I sat; she shuffled; I cut.

"Maybe I'll find out another time," I said. "I'm on my way to
bed and only obeying an impulse. One hand." I put a hundred-
dollar chip on the table.

She dealt me a pair of red aces and herself the ♠2 up. I smiled
and split the bullets, digging a Benjamin Franklin out of my
pocket and sliding it under the chip. She slid me an eight and
a nine and the Tingle returned in earnest. She flipped her down
card, the ♠4, and topped it with the ♠5, the ♠3, and finally, like
a fish hook from the card gods inserted somewhat below the
base of the spine, the ♠7!

Nineteen and twenty, *and* two hundred dollars, eaten by a
five-flush twenty-one in spades! A four hundred dollar swing.
The Tingle laughed at me. I sat stunned. I looked at the redhead.

Her expression seemed genuinely and helplessly apologetic. Either that or she could act as good as she looked. She shrugged and took my money.

"Wiss, you jerk," a voice stated from directly over my left shoulder.

"Alan, jeez!" I exclaimed, swivelling around.

"Never seen a blackjack hand so diabolic," the Shadow said. " Even to the downside rush you must have felt when the five gave her eleven. Maybe if you'd been dealt *two* nines..."

"I think it's the card gods telling me to stick to bridge this week. How are *you?* When'd you get in?"

"Five minutes ago. Left San Francisco after dinner and drove in with my client. Speaking of that, make sure you call me (censored) this week."

"Of course. It took you eight hours from the coast?"

"The pass is snowed under. We needed chains."

"Your client doesn't like to fly?"

"You guessed it. He only attends tournaments he can get to by wheel."

"You going to have much free time?"

"Maybe one evening. The mornings depend on the knock-outs. I expect we can have a few breakfasts later in the week."

"Which evening? Maybe we can hit a show."

"How about some rubber instead? Our whole team would rather do that."

"How about both? An early show, and rubber after if you're already out of the K.O.'s?"

"Sold. I'll let you know. Feel like a bite to eat?"

"No, I'm wasted. And after that last hand more than a little depressed."

Alan chuckled. "So get some sleep. How about if I try to rustle up a rubber for tomorrow afternoon as well? I can't think of a better way to spend Christmas Day in Reno."

"Nor can I," I said.

A few minutes later I poured myself into bed, thinking that Santa would be near to finishing his rounds. I hoped he'd stuff my stockings with the dainty feet of the redhead, but failing that, perhaps bring me some good cards for the afternoon. I needed a change.

* * *

I awoke to the jarring ring of the telephone at precisely the crack of noon.

"Wiss, you jerk," it spoke, "are you still asleep?"

"Hell, no. I'm making somnambulism an art form."

"Well, step in a cold shower and get your act down to the coffee shop. The rubber's on right after breakfast and I want you to meet the guys'n'girl before we start."

"Girl?" I mumbled.

"My client's girl, and she's a dish. You try to behave yourself."

"Alan, I've never aced out another guy unless it was the lady's idea. What Lola wants, Lola gets, no?"

"Most definitely no. And make sure that shower's *damn* cold." The line clicked and hollowed.

The shower was warm. Did the Shadow think me a masochist?

Alan's client was a man of considerable means not given to hiding the fact. Gold and crystallised carbon adorned his fingers, wrists, and neck, and imported silks clothed a body that had long since succumbed to gravity. His face bore a continual expression of wide-eyed puzzlement, as if wondering where the heck middle age had gone and how had it ever slipped by him. He had all his hair, much to my envy, but it was coloured by vanity to the bootblack barf of Grecian Formula. Next to the baldies who let the hair over one ear grow to half a foot so they can plaster a few strands like worms with rigor mortis over their pates, I find few acts of vanity more obvious, more disgusting, or more futile. He insisted I call him Hal, not Harold, and tried his best to crush a bone or two when we shook hands. Having met the type before, I was ready for his grip.

I was not, however, ready for his girlfriend.

Dish of cream is an understatement, without any further references which would simply appear as the sexist male droolings they are. Perhaps a third of Hal's age, a half of his weight, and a full portion of his vanity, she greeted me with slightly lowered lids, a waft of intoxicating perfume, and a hand that slid into mine like an eel into seaweed. She called herself Ginger, which fit as close as the white knit dress she wore. I played a guessing game with myself as to whether she was a hired pro or simply a serious fortune hunter and Hal's answer to male menopause.

"Siddown, siddown," Hal motioned. "Larry and Dave are at the tables; you'll meet them later."

I sat across from Hal, between Ginger and Alan, hardly settling before I felt a warm pressure against my knee.

The devil and the deep blue sea, dammit. I wanted to return the pressure and I wanted to run for my life. Compromising, even with myself, I reached into my pocket for a smoke and crossed my legs. It was apparent she wasn't a pro, because a pro wouldn't ask me for the time of day with her johnny at her side. That made her Hal's answer to the youth fountain, who was looking for a little more youth on her own. It also made her capital tee Trouble.

"Larry and Dave are the other half of your team?" I asked Hal. Oblivious to the obvious.

"Yeah. And not a bad pair. I think with (censored, yet again) here we stand a chance, certainly in the Swiss if not the K.O.'s."

"Well, I wish you luck," I said, as silk-covered toes tickled my ankles.

"Merry Christmas!" a cheery voice spoke over my right shoulder. "What'll it be, folks?" Saved by the waitress. I turned, again severing Ginger contact, and ordered breakfast with the group. It was pleasant enough, consisting mostly of small talk and face filling, with the only real difficulty being eye contact with Ginger when we spoke. She was too young to really know discretion, and was unable to keep either the heat or the amusement from her eyes. Hal seemed oblivious, only paying attention to her when he referred to her, like the pig he was. Alan, on the other hand, didn't miss an iota. Once he cracked my right ankle while she was tickling my left, nearly causing me to choke on a piece of toast.

Timely, Larry and Dave arrived when the coffee did. Hal made the introductions, ordered more coffee, and pulled up a couple of extra chairs. Gratefully I pulled myself closer to Alan to make room for Dave, who was still cursing his luck at the tables. He got little sympathy from me, of course, and Alan was quick to tell him of the diabolic spade hand that had done me in the night before.

To my relief, for almost every time I glanced at Ginger she was looking at me, breakfast was soon over and we were on our way up to Hal's suite for some five-wheel Chicago. Ginger disappeared into the bowels of the hotel, credit card from Hal in hand, as we stepped into the elevator. I hoped she was a slow and thorough shopper.

* * *

I was lucky enough to cut the deuce of diamonds, which sat me out for the first round and allowed me time for a calming detour on the balcony, where I smoked a cold shower. When I stepped back in Dave was already dealing the third hand, simultaneously breathing fire across the table at Larry, whose lower lip flapped protrusively: "...but, but, but..."

"Did you think there were fourteen clubs in the deck?" Dragon Dave snapped. "Maybe we forgot to take out the joker."

I helped myself to a drink and seated myself between Dave and Alan.

DRAGON DAVE
♠ A K x
♡ x
♢ x x
♣ K J T 9 x x x

ALAN
♠ Q T 7 x
♡ A x x
♢ K Q J x
♣ x x

Dave opened one club at unfavourable, Hal doubled, and Larry's lip was right in there with one heart. Another pinochle deck, I thought, considering the cuebid of two hearts probably best. Alan didn't think so. He simply bid game in spades. That got passed around to Larry who was right there with five clubs. Alan doubled, and poor Hal went into a stew of his own making, emerging with a tortured five spades. That got passed back to Dave who breathed fire with *his* double.

Not quite the way Mister Binsky prefers to get to the five level, I don't think.

"Is that a penalty double?" Larry the Lip cracked, and led the heart queen out of turn.

"Can't you pay attention to the goddam auction?" Dave blustered.

"What do you want to do, partner?" Hal asked. Since those were the days prior to the rule change that would have permitted Alan to choose to accept the lead and lay his own hand down as dummy, thereby making Hal boil in his own cauldron, he simply applied Goldwater's Rule, accepting, but looking at Hal's dummy before he played to the trick from his hand.

HAL
♠ 9 x x x
♡ K T 9 8
◇ A T 9 x x
♣ -

LARRY THE LIP
♠ J 8
♡ Q J x x x
◇ x x
♣ A Q x x

When Hal put his dummy down it was clear why he had been so pained to hear Alan double five clubs. Even Plum Meredith would not have been proud of that spade suit. No mention was made of the fact the hand was at least an ace short of a takeout double. Perhaps that's because the shape and texture were so good.

Alan won the king of hearts on the table and played a spade to the eight, ten, and king. Helpless, Dave pumped the dummy with a club. Another spade went to the jack, queen, and ace. Dave pumped the dummy's last trump, but Alan had a diamond entry to his hand to draw Dave's last one, and he claimed.

"Nice lead, Lar'," Dave said.

"It didn't matter," Alan cut in. "It's cold on any lead from either side. Pure luck."

I had seen only one hand, but if it were any indication of normal team behaviour I figured Alan would have his mornings free very quickly.

Hal dealt the fourth hand, opening one diamond, passed by the Lip to Alan's ♠AKxx ♡KTx ◇- ♣Qxxxxx. Alan bid two clubs, pass by Dave, and Hal quietly rebid *five* diamonds. Alan thought about it for a moment, then raised to *six* diamonds on his void! Hal held: ♠x ♡Axx ◇AKxxxxxx ♣A, diamonds were 3-2 and the hand was a spread.

"Nice bid," Hal said.

"I always wanted to bid a slam on a void," Alan answered. "This seemed like the right one for it. Mikey's in; Dave's out. Larry and I switch."

I sat down, took the cut from the Lip, and dealt the cards, pleased I was starting with the Shadow as my partner. This was the first hand:

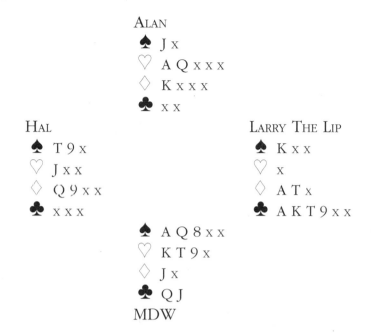

Alan
♠ J x
♡ A Q x x x
◇ K x x x
♣ x x

Hal
♠ T 9 x
♡ J x x
◇ Q 9 x x
♣ x x x

Larry The Lip
♠ K x x
♡ x
◇ A T x
♣ A K T 9 x x

♠ A Q 8 x x
♡ K T 9 x
◇ J x
♣ Q J
MDW

My hand may have been a dog thirteen, with the quack and jack, but I preferred to look at it as a great nine and get right in there with one spade. Hal passed, Alan bid one no trump, and the Lip came in with two clubs. I bid two hearts, and Alan raised me to game. The Lip doubled! What is this, matchpoints? I thought as the dummy appeared on Hal's club lead.

The Lip cashed two clubs, thought about it, and switched to a trump. When he subsequently covered the jack of spades I was doomed. Just my luck. He could have led any card from any suit in his hand and I was cold, except for the trump switch. He could have had one fewer trump and been endplayed at trick three. Was this simply not my lucky day, or did I push too much?

"Nice switch, Larry," I said.

"Too bad Dave missed it," he answered. "He gripes when I'm wrong and says zip when I'm right. Sometimes he even gripes when *he's* wrong."

"Well, we've all been victim to that one. It's our own ego kicking us in the ass, even when we know we're wrong. *Especially* when we know. My guess is he also knows you've been patient with him, even if he's never acknowledged it."

"You a psychiatrist or something?" Hal piped in as he dealt.

"He's definitely a something," Alan said. "What.. is not entirely clear."

Then Alan wound up playing a no trump game with these cards:

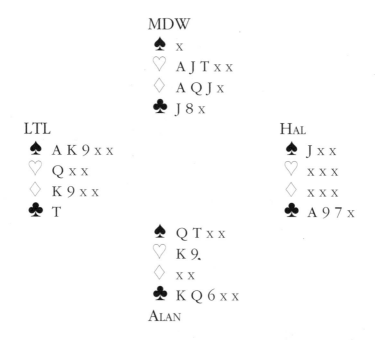

MDW
♠ x
♡ A J T x x
◇ A Q J x
♣ J 8 x

LTL
♠ A K 9 x x
♡ Q x x
◇ K 9 x x
♣ T

HAL
♠ J x x
♡ x x x
◇ x x x
♣ A 9 7 x

♠ Q T x x
♡ K 9.
◇ x x
♣ K Q 6 x x
ALAN

The Lip opened one spade and after I doubled Alan ended up in three no trump, with a low spade lead to Hal's jack and Alan's queen. Alan considered the hand and emerged with the nine of hearts. The Lip looked at it and covered with the lady.

"Nice play," said Alan.

Had the Lip ducked Alan would have floated the nine, then, still in his hand, hooked the diamond. Back to the king of hearts, another diamond finesse, and nine tricks. The Lip's cover had effectively removed one of Alan's entries for the two diamond finesses he needed. Now Alan changed tact. He played back to his hand with the heart king and took one diamond hook. Then he ran all his hearts to this position:

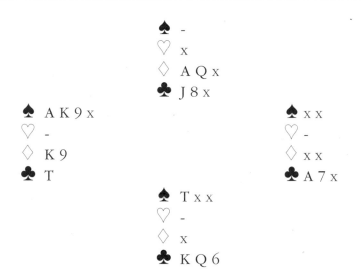

On the last heart Hal and Alan pitched diamonds, and the Lip was in a quandary. If he threw his club, Alan would play ace and another diamond, and the spade ten would become the ninth trick. A diamond pitch was unthinkable, and throwing a spade would enable Alan to lead a club safely. Larry eventually shrugged and threw in his cards.

"What the hell are you doin'?!" Hal exclaimed.

"Conceding," Larry said. "I'm strip-squeezed in three suits. Unless you're holding the ten of spades and falsecarded me at trick one?" He raised an eyebrow.

"I've got it," Alan said, showing his hand. "There's no way to beat it, 'though you gave it a good try."

"Interesting hand to play in five clubs," I said, having thought about it while dummying up. "Care to play or defend?"

"I care to play the next one," Hal grumbled. "C'mon, deal," he said to Alan.

So the Shadow dealt.

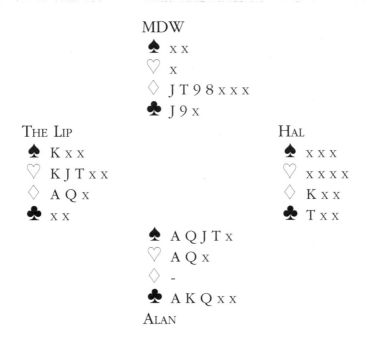

MDW
♠ x x
♡ x
♢ J T 9 8 x x x
♣ J 9 x

THE LIP
♠ K x x
♡ K J T x x
♢ A Q x
♣ x x

HAL
♠ x x x
♡ x x x x
♢ K x x
♣ T x x

♠ A Q J T x
♡ A Q x
♢ -
♣ A K Q x x
ALAN

Alan hates to open two clubs on two suiters, and true to form started with one club. Larry overcalled one heart, I lamented my garbage, and Hal stuffed in a two heart call on *his* crud. Over Alan's two spades the Lip rebid hearts, and it was back to Alan. He bid the spade game, and when I quietly preferred clubs he raised himself to slam. That was too much for the Lip. He doubled and led the jack of hearts. After all, his partner had raised him.

The play took only seconds.

Alan won the queen and ace of hearts, dumping a spade, ruffed his last heart, led a spade to the ace and followed with the queen. The Lip covered, Alan ruffed with the nine, cashed the jack, ruffed himself back to hand with a diamond, and laid down the top trumps, claiming with an overtrick.

"What the hell did you double on?" Hal growled.

"The same thing I led a heart with," The Lip answered. "Your bid on air."

"Easy on the acrimony, gentlemen," Alan said, cutting for the Lip. "It affects the bouquet of this excellent scotch."

Pouting, Larry dealt a beauty for me.

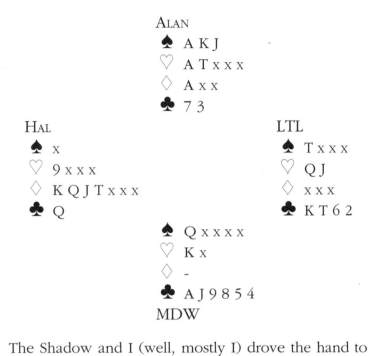

ALAN
♠ A K J
♡ A T x x x
♢ A x x
♣ 7 3

HAL
♠ x
♡ 9 x x x
♢ K Q J T x x x
♣ Q

LTL
♠ T x x x
♡ Q J
♢ x x x
♣ K T 6 2

♠ Q x x x x
♡ K x
♢ -
♣ A J 9 8 5 4
MDW

The Shadow and I (well, mostly I) drove the hand to six clubs, Hal preempting in diamonds along the way. He led the king, and as I stared at the dummy Ginger walked in followed by a bellhop laden with treasure.

"Hi, fellas," she said, heading for the bedroom. "Hal, baby, will you tip this nice young man?" Wiggle, wiggle.

Not being Terence Reese, I was unable to ignore her. Neither was anyone else, I was happy to see.

The bellhop put the packages on the couch as Hal obediently dug into a pocket and found a five dollar chip.

"Here, kid," he said, flipping it. The bellhop's hand snatched it from the air like a frog's tongue with a fly, and with a quick 'thankyousir' he was gone. I went back to studying the hand.

Winning the diamond ace, I pitched a spade, then floated the seven of clubs. Hal gobbled up the trick with his stiff queen and led another top diamond. I ruffed, entered dummy with a spade to the ace, and played a club to the eight, Hal donating another diamond. Another spade to the king and another diamond ruff and I was finally shortened to the same number of trumps as the Lip. At this point he counted down to 4-2-3-4.

Also at this point Ginger returned to the room and seated herself between Hal and me. One heady waft of perfume and I had to recount the hand. Fortunately it was Mikey proof. A spade to the jack, heart to the king, spade queen cash and heart to dummy's ace left my trump tenace sitting over the Lip. He conceded.

"Well stroked," Alan said.

"What if Hal doesn't help you shorten yourself at trick three?" Larry asked.

"No matter, I still have the entries."

"I wish *I* knew how to play," Ginger pouted, "but Hal won't teach me."

He won't pay me to teach you either, I thought.

"There's lots of books on the subject," I said cowardly. All right, then. Disc*reet*ly.

The game went on. We played through the afternoon, ordered food to the room, and continued playing well into Christmas Eve. Ginger, knowing full well I was not immune to her, continued her little acts of coquetry. She always seated herself next to Hal, which, when I partnered him, left her in the perfect position to give me meaningful, if slightly bovine, stares. She also crossed and recrossed her legs a bit more slowly and a bit more often than when she was seated beside me.

The next time I sat out I went through the bedroom for a leak break, and when I left the bathroom she just happened to be waiting to get in, timing her entrance so she had to pass close to me. Quite close.

About zero inches, if you really want to take a measurement.

I refuse to believe that all of these distractions would not have affected even Mister Reese. Certainly *my* concentration went over the balcony more than once, and I blew the play and defense on hands I would have worked out had I been paying enough attention to them.

Alan raised an eyebrow at me on a few occasions, finally suggesting during a late balcony break that we call it a night, for bridge anyway.

"You stroked a couple of those dummies like they were made of broken glass," he said.

"No kidding," I agreed. "Well, I've certainly had enough. At this point I'm ready to take on that redheaded blackjack dealer again. In more ways than one."

"How many outfits has Ginger modelled anyway?"

"What makes you think I counted?"

"What makes me think the sun'll come up tomorrow?"

"Four."

"Let's get out here."

We broke up the game to only minor protests from the Dragon and the Lip. Hal had had enough of everything, and was beginning to look a little fuzzy around the edges. Ginger said she was going to tuck him in and ushered him to the bedroom, casting me a meaningful and indiscrete glance over her shoulder. If Dave or Larry noticed they gave no sign.

Minutes later Alan and I were back in the casino.

"How about coffee and a piece of fruit pie?" he asked. "A little energy before hitting the tables."

We'd hardly begun to sip before Ginger appeared at our side.

"Hal's asleep. Out like a light," she said, fluttering an eyelash or two. "Mind if I join you?" And she slipped in beside me before we could answer.

I wish I could find restaurants with coffee as hot as the thigh that pressed against mine, but then coffee doesn't cost as much, does it?

Twenty uncomfortable minutes later Alan stood up.

"Well," he said to Ginger, "we're going to hit the tables."

"O, let me join you! Hal gave me some cash to gamble." She smiled at me. I was having a little trouble getting up. I mean standing up.

"Actually, we're going downtown," I lied. "The rules are a little more flexible in some places."

"That's great. I'd love to get out of here for a while."

"Well, uh, Ginger..." Alan hibbered, and lied through his teeth, "...after that we were going to take a cab out to Mustang..."

"O!" she exclaimed. "O. Well, I couldn't get involved in *that*. I guess I'll leave you guys to do your guy things." She shook her head, gave me a look of undisguised disapproval, said goodnight, and was gone.

"Thanks, buddy," I said as we left the restaurant.

"Think nothing of it. Just try to work out how you're going to avoid her for the *rest* of the week!"

The Shadow and I drifted along the blackjack tables, looking for the redhead with the smile in her eyes and the devil in her cards.

Shadow Wasted in the Desert Air

THE SEPTEMBER SKY OF PALM SPRINGS was cloudless as normal. Unfortunately its blue was no longer pristine, as over the years the grundge enveloping the Los Angeles basin had crept through the San Berdoo valley and over the lower peaks of the San Gabriels. It's a perfect time to hold a bridge tournament, between the oven-like heat of the summer and the gouging hotel rates of the winter season.

I had planned a visit to my grandfather to coincide with the 1992 Palm Springs regional. As it happened, at the age of ninety-nine and change, he had to undergo a major operation, and was convalescing when I arrived, necessitating enough of my attention that I managed only one day of play and a few sessions of kibitzing during the tournament. He had lost his enthusiasm for bridge at ninety-six, when my grandmother, his lifelong partner, went to the club where finesses only lose when they guarantee the contract. His urge for poker with his cronies waned prior to his illness, perhaps influenced by his young ladyfriend of early eighty-something, but he still has a soft spot for a hand or two of rummy. He doesn't hold his cards too well anymore, but it hardly matters. His luck, uncanny when I was a teenager, hadn't deserted him. He won enough to tip his haircut lady.

*　*　*

One of the major advantages of kibitzing – other than self-improvement – is that while a declarer or defender is thinking about a play that you already know will or will not work, you can glance around the room, playing your personal version of People-Watch. It was while in such a mode that for the first time in my life I spotted the Shadow before he spotted me.

I was kibitzing my buddy Bobby Levin; his left-hand opponent was on play and deep in thought, and I let my eyes stray around the room, the better not to be bored watching the gears clash in the brain-on-play. A dapper fellow, well-tanned and sporting a thick salt and pepper moustache, stood from a nearby table and walked out of the room, passing within ten feet of me. There was no doubt about it. Despite his disguise, I knew it was my longtime friend, Alan. The Shadow.

It is not good policy to interrupt one's kibitzing during the play of a hand, no matter how simple or foregone the conclusion, so I waited until the declarer had painstakingly extricated every card from hand, like barbed thorns from thumb, then excused myself from the table.

A quick check of the hall and the washroom showed them both to be Shadowless. That left the smoking area, which in Palm Springs, like an increasing amount of tournaments, meant outdoors. I rounded a corner and found Alan leaning against a wall, grinning at me.

"What took you so long?" he asked.

"Expletive deleted," I answered as we greeted. " You *did* spot me first!"

"Yesterday. You were kibitzing Levin then too. But you were gone before I could get to you."

"Spending time with my Zaida in Palm Desert."

"He's well I hope?"

"Pretty good, considering. Desert air agrees with him. What's with this Mister Desert Man disguise? You look like a Sonny Bono yes man."

"Cute, isn't it?" He spread his arms, looking down at himself. "It's my own damn fault. I was in Vegas, playing some poker, playing some golf. Somewhere in the chatter I mentioned bridge. Big mistake. Deep Pockets, my partner here, donated pretty substantially into my coffers both at the table and on the course, and he liked my act enough to smile when he paid up, so when he told me there was a tournament in Palm Springs and insisted I play with him I couldn't turn him down. Fortunately there aren't a lot of pros here, so nobody's recognised me. Passell would probably see through this but I've been keeping out of his way, making sure we never play in the same section in opposite directions. If we meet in a team match I'm going to have to wear shades and hope for the best. How do you like the hairpiece?"

"The one on your head or your upper lip?"

"Listen, I have to get back in. Meet me after the session."

"Can't. I'll be with my grandfather."

"Then tell me where you're staying. I'll drop by after the evening session."

* * *

Late that evening as I was lounging under the stars and palms I heard in the quiet night the unmistakable squish of a Shadow on damp grass.

"Hi, Alan," I said, a moment before he rounded the corner.

"Just what I expected to find," he said. "Wiss wasted in the desert air. And blessed with tunnel hearing, no doubt."

"It wasn't your aftershave. Make yourself comfortable. How'd it go today?"

"With no small dose of amazement. Got any brew?"

"Inside. Little fridge in the corner. I picked up a six-pack of the preferred."

"O, you are a thoughtful fellow," he said as he disappeared into the room. He was back in a moment with a cold one. "You remember a poem about a cactus flower blooming with its sweetness wasted on the desert air? Unlike you, of course," he punctuated with the hiss of escaping beer gas as he popped the tin.

"The bloom whose odour no one is around to appreciate. Like the unheard tree falling. Sure."

"Well, the cactus bloomed twice today. The first time was when you found me outside this afternoon. I'd gone there to count to ten ten times. The second was about a half hour ago. I'm glad the session was almost over. Then Deep Pockets didn't believe I was meeting a friend. Kept thinking I had a rendezvous lined up with (censored), and he wanted to join the fun. Nudge nudge wink wink. She was doing nothing more at the table than just being friendly. The guy can be a real pain."

"So you were either defending or dummy."

"What makes you think I wasn't declaring?"

"Because the only unsmelled rose on play would be lousy defense, letting you make a hand easily and denying you a coup. Partner, as dummy, can have very little effect. Therefore, either you were defending, and Deep Pockets denied you his cooperation, or you were dummy, and a hand offered you a rarity, like a Devil's Coup, and you had to watch your partner botch the play of it. My guess is both hands are the former, because only if you were directly involved with your partner would you be so frustrated."

"Mikey, that's quite astute."

"Comes as a bonus with the tunnel hearing. Think nothing of it."

"All right. You hold ♠A8x ♡Kx ♢AKxxx ♣KTx. First you get to bid it."

"I'm going to defend with this hand?"

"Sorry. Everybody's hot. You're up, weak notrumps. Colonial Acol."

"Where'd you find this guy?"

"Bid."

"I'll try one of my suit."

"Lefty passes, partner raises to two as a noisemaker, and righty, whom I should categorise as competent but inexpert, bids three of your suit after a moment's thought. Now what?"

"The first thing that occurs is three notrump, but that can't be right."

"Why not?"

"I need partner to have the ♣AJ along with the diamonds coming in. Not too likely. I guess double shows my hand."

"This goes to righty who bids four spades. You lead a top diamond and dummy tables ♠Tx ♡98x ♢T9xx ♣98xx . Your partner puts the queen under your lead and declarer lapses into a coma for a full three minutes. When he emerges he ruffs with the *king* of spades and leads the queen! Defend."

"So he wants a dummy entry with the ten of spades. What's good for declarer is not so good for you, so the natural inclination is to duck."

"Do you?"

"Not when you've got that glint in your eye. Let me think about it."

"Think all you want. You can even have as long as the inexpert declarer." A Cheshire grin widened on his face.

"Would you like a tissue?" I asked. "I'm sure that's suds and not sarcasm drooling from the corner of your mouth."

"Now you're stalling. C'mon. This is a good hand."

"All right, all right. Let's see... He's advertised the majors and chosen spades himself. He's probably 6-5-0-2. If he were 6-6-0-1 he might have redoubled three diamonds or even recued four diamonds to force a preference from his partner."

"So far so good."

"So our defensive tricks are a spade, a heart, and a club. I don't see what this play of ruffing with the king is all about. His suit can't be any worse than KQJ9xx or he's chancing to promote A8xx in my hand. Why didn't he just ruff low and lead a spade at the ten if he wanted a dummy entry?" I looked for a hint, but the Shadow just shrugged and mugged another grin at me.

"Okay," I continued. "Maybe in his mind my partner's raise was based on the diamond quack and the spade ace. So what are declarer's hearts then? They can't be as good as AQJxx. The hand's cold even if he never sees dummy. Jeez, I've already thought about this so long even a troglodyte can work out my partner doesn't have the ace! All right, take away his jack of hearts. Now he needs the heart hook. I think I'm getting it now. If he places me with the king of hearts he has no option but to play ace and another and hope the king is dubby, which it happens to be. So now it looks right to win the spade and give him the entry so he can lose the hook. Then we get two heart tricks." I smiled. Alan stared at me blankly.

"I'm missing something," I said. He shrugged again, pursed his lips. Now I was *certain* I'd missed something. "Clubs? He must have the ace and another or he's more than inexpert; he's a raving maniac...."

"You're close, Mikey. Not to the answer, of course, but to the key to it."

"Which is the nearest thing to a hint I'm going to get from you. So I've given partner the jack third of hearts and declarer ace queen fifth," I went on, "dummy has nine eight ex... where the heck's the ten?! The ten of hearts!" The Shadow allowed a slight smile. "Declarer's got it. I see it now. He's on a heart guess. Either ace and out, catering to the existing situation, or ace and queen, trying to smother a dubby jack. If he gets to dummy he can float the heart nine. If it loses to the jack he can try the ace next. That works if partner has king dubby or I have king dubby or king jack tight. But then it's better for him to cash the heart ace before he goes to dummy to lead a heart up. So either way he's likely to go right. Where the hell's the fourth trick coming from, anyway? Thin air?"

The Shadow laughed. "Bingo," he said.

"Bingo? Thin air? We're getting the setting trick from thin air?" Once again I was looking at a poker face. "I don't get it."

"Wanna give up?"

"What, when I'm so close? We're double dummy now."

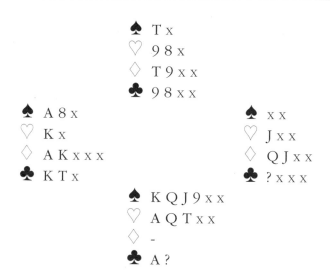

```
                    ♠ T x
                    ♡ 9 8 x
                    ◇ T 9 x x
                    ♣ 9 8 x x
♠ A 8 x                            ♠ x x
♡ K x                             ♡ J x x
◇ A K x x x                       ◇ Q J x x
♣ K T x                           ♣ ? x x x
                    ♠ K Q J 9 x x
                    ♡ A Q T x x
                    ◇ -
                    ♣ A ?
```

"Partner must have the queen of clubs for his raise, maybe the jack as well, although that can hardly matter."

"All right. Give him the queen. Anything come to mind now?"

I studied the hand. "A trick out of thin air, on a cold hand, with fruitless minors. If we can't get two tricks in hearts the only other possibility is spades... and that means a heart ruff!"

"Bravo," Alan said, tapping his brew on the table. "Now engineer it."

"All right. Let's see... jeez, I love this Sherlock stuff! Okay, okay. To get the ruff I need two things, namely to shorten my hearts to zero, and having done that, to get to partner's hand. I think I see it. I win the ace of spades, giving him his entry, and I put the king of clubs down. No. That doesn't work. Declarer just ducks and we're helpless."

"I told you declarer's no expert. He wins the ace of clubs and enters dummy with a trump to the ten. What do you think he thinks your hand is?"

"Diamond ace king, spade ace, club king *queen,* and maybe even jack! He thinks partner has *both* heart honours and the diamond quack for his raise."

"Bingo again. He floats the nine of hearts."

"I duck."

"He leads the heart eight. Partner plays the jack, his known card, declarer the queen, and you your timely king."

"And now I lead the club ten to partner's queen for the heart ruff!" I concluded proudly. Then I noticed the Shadow's face. It looked as if it had been whipped with the Louisville Slugger of outrageous fortune.

"O no," I said, "Don't tell me Deep Pockets had the jack of clubs and didn't overtake the ten!"

"Okay, I won't tell you. Actually, declarer held the club ace jack tight."

"Then what happened?"

"When he led the eight of hearts Deep Pockets neglected to cover with the jack..."

"And he diagnosed the situation and dropped your king!"

"Worse. He thought about it for a while, then decided to play me for only two trumps and partner for an idiot who didn't play a heart honour the second time to guarantee himself a trick. He floated the eight, I won the king, played the club ten to partner's queen, and even when he saw the jack appear from declarer's hand he tried to give me a *club* ruff! A Magician's Coup, a trick from thin air where there never was one. Thin wasted desert air!"

"My consolation," I said, "but the only important thing about it proves again how often Shakespeare was right."

"Come again?"

"'The play's the thing', Alan. You made the play. It's worth another brew."

"I accept. You fetch."

It took me only a few moments to return, but by then Alan had already finished scrawling half a deck on the inside of an unused scorecard. He exchanged it for the beer.

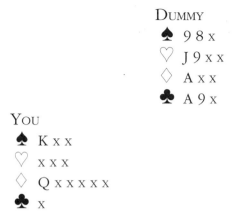

Dummy
♠ 9 8 x
♡ J 9 x x
◇ A x x
♣ A 9 x

You
♠ K x x
♡ x x x
◇ Q x x x x x
♣ x

"This time you're in first at favourable. You pass, lefty starts with one spade, and partner, the inimitable Deep Pockets, doubles. I should forewarn you that with him a double seems to show any twelve points and any thirteen cards. Righty bids two notrump, which is alerted as a spade limit raise. Your spade king appears to be worth bupkus, so you bid four diamonds in case your partner knows what to do with a suggestion. Lefty bids four spades as expected, and partner comes in with five diamonds. When righty passes this, lefty's five spades ends the auction. Partner leads the jack of diamonds and declarer wins the ace. Once more it's up to you." He sat back and began sipping.

"Do I get to see only three cards of this trick or am I entitled to know what declarer plays?"

"I was wondering when you were going to ask. You tell me."

"Well, since partner rates to have KJTx my guess is declarer pitches a rounded card."

"Heart spot, actually. Now what?"

"Now I have to think about it. Declarer's got a lot of clubs, for sure. Partner has king or queen fourth, so that leaves a five-bagger for declarer. He can't be happy with the Binsky level with terrible texture in the suit, so it's unlikely partner has a slow trick even with the ten. We have nothing coming in diamonds and it looks as if the same is true for hearts. Declarer probably started with Ax. So he'd be 6-2-0-5. Maybe I should have saved in six diamonds, is what I think. Why didn't partner lead the heart king anyway?"

"Why not, indeed?" Alan said. There was that glint in his eye again.

"Because he didn't have it! Declarer must have started with AKx in hearts, which leaves partner with QTx. So partner is either 1-3-4-5 or 2-3-4-4, and declarer 6-3-0-4 or 5-3-0-5. To have any kind of a double partner must have the spade ace! I've got it now. I fly with the king when a trump comes off dummy! If partner's ace is stiff I apologise and scrape the egg off my face, otherwise I switch to my club and when partner wins the next trump I get my ruff. How'd I do?"

"You did fine. Like me you were minus six fifty."

"Six fifty? I don't get it. If I crashed the ace we should be minus six eighty."

"You didn't crash it, but you did take as long to play to trick one as I did. By the time I turned my card everybody at the table but me had forgotten which hand was on play. Before I could stop anyone declarer had played the spade queen from his hand, and partner in a flash had his ace on it to start a meaningless pump in diamonds!"

"It *was* stiff," I said.

"Like hell it was," the Shadow muttered through some froth. "It was just another cactus flower. What would Wee Willie say about that?"

"He'd commiserate, no doubt, and say all who play this game will at some time suffer the slings and arrows of outrageous partners."

"He'd be right again. Say, you suppose I could slip into that hot tub at this hour?"

"The management has been asleep since ten. I won't tell if you don't."

In a moment the Shadow was in his shorts, heading for the tub. "If I should slip below the surface, just ignore me," he said over his shoulder. "Either I've drowned or I'm checking to see if this rug floats off, and which one it may be is entirely irrelevant."

Shadow at the Country Club

THE EIGHTEENTH WAS A STRAIGHTAWAY four par that was normally nothing more than a drive and a mid to short iron. Trees and long rough line the fairway, and a few small bunkers dot the right side, short of the landing area but perfectly placed to punish the simple club player who can't fly a drive two and a quarter or keep it low where the prevailing breeze can't push it into the sand.

. This, however, was anything but a normal day, with winds gusting to near gale force and on this hole, straight in our faces. I hate the wind. Golfing in the British Isles has never been an ambition of mine, and never will be. I had thought golfing in British Columbia would be relatively safe, 'though, so I agreed to let the Shadow spot me three strokes too many and pass a morning on the links of a country club where the members were under the erroneous impression that I was one of them. If the club pro had any suspicions he laid them aside when he recognised Alan, in his not-too-invisible guise as sometime touring pro (censored). He was delighted to find us an opening (not too difficult, considering the wind conditions), and allow us to play as a twosome.

"I think we should skip this one and go directly to the nineteenth," I suggested.

"Courage, Mikey," Alan said. "It's taken you sixteen holes to regain the honour; this is hardly the time to relinquish it."

"Sez you." On the holes where the wind came across the fairway in one way or another my tee shots simply followed it in whatever the appropriate direction might be. One tree or bush is very much like another. On those where it was at my back, I hit my tee shots a ton, far past any place on the fairway where I was familiar with the approach. Invariably I misclubbed and overshot the green.

But with the wind in my face...

Adventureland. The Twilight Zone. And most assuredly, a crap shoot.

"Just a smooth deuce," Alan said. "A little off the inside foot to keep it low and let the club do the work. It'll bore right through that breeze."

"Sez you," I repeated, addressing the ball and doing my waggle. I swung.

Dead solid perfect. I couldn't remember the last time I'd struck a ball so pure. It started low and stayed there. If only I hadn't had the clubface just a *little* open, enabling that blasted breeze to blow the ball just a *little* right.

So that like a rifle shot it drove on a line into one of those pot bunkers and buried itself a foot below the lip. I could see the dimple from the tee. I swear the wind brought the plop back to me in laughter.

"No golf god," Alan said, biting his lip. He duplicated my shot, without the open clubface.

I was fortunate to reach the green in par. Two routine putts for a double-bogey and I was heading for the nineteenth before Alan had tapped in his four. He caught up to me as I was cleaning my spikes.

"Wanna go another nine?" he asked.

"In your dreams."

"How about lunch?"

"Dining up. Coffee shop down."

"Down. All I want is a soup and sand."

"I *knew* you were going to bring up sand again," I muttered. Alan allowed a slight smile.

We changed shoes and headed for the coffee shop, soon passing a small, glass-encircled room. Inside were a half dozen tables filled with foursomes, and none of them were playing golf.

"Will you have a look at that?" Alan jerked a thumb.

"Yup. They're at it seven days a week," I said, quickening my pace.

"How about a little entertainment after lunch? My plane doesn't leave till after five." Slow to take a hint, the Shadow.

"How about a movie? Your choice."

"I choose bridge. Come on. Those old gents in there look like they'd be fun."

"If your idea of fun is traipsing through the tulips in the Twilight Zone, then I'm in full agreement."

"You've played in that game?"

"Only once."

"Mikey, how bad can it be?"

"It's not that it's bad. Almost all the gents in there are just that - gentlemen, although there is an exception or two. It's not that, and it's not the quality of the game. It's simply that I can't play while listening to all the drivel between, and sometimes during the hands. Trust me. It's no different than the ladies' game; these guys yak just as much, and make only half as much sense. The rewards aren't worth it."

"Rewards? What are the stakes here?"

"Two bits, but I wasn't talking monetary..."

"Twenty-five cents a point is a fairly steep game."

"Alan, that's twenty-five cents a *hundred* ."

"O. I see."

* * *

We drifted into the card room. I knew that soup and a sandwich was not enough to fortify me for the game, but I agreed to hang around and kibitz the Shadow.

"In case you need to be carried out," I said.

As we arrived the General was admonishing his rabbit of the moment in stentorian tones audible halfway down the hall.

The General was the acknowledged expert of the country club, an imposing non-gentleman septuagenarian with selective hearing and eagle eyesight who was built like Ichabod Crane with muscles. He was the proud holder of more than two hundred master points, ten times that of the rest of the club members combined. The selective hearing came in handy when the General needed time to think in the bidding. True to his personality he never asked anyone to repeat their bid; he just bellowed, "Speak up, goddammit!" The eagle eyesight came in handy when taking the odd balcony finesse.

"He's not a bad dummy player," I told the Shadow. "That and intimidation are his strongest points. He can't bid worth a crap, 'though. The usual notrump hog, regardless of distribution, and usually an ace to an ace and a king overstated in values. He's no help in the defense, either. Scrambles his carding all the time, trying to fool opposition who never look at the cards and only confusing partners who do. Of course, that gives him more ammunition when they screw up. That it was his fault for putting them in a guessing position when he could have made the defense clear is irrelevant."

"Well," Alan said, "looks like that's the game I should cut into."

"By all means," I said. "From a kibitzer's viewpoint nothing could be better."

"Hey, boys," someone piped up from a corner table,"look who's here! It's (censored once again)!"

There was a short interruption of the games in progress for some handshakes and welcomes as the club members greeted the arrival of a minor golf celebrity. After that it was no trouble cutting into the General's game after only a short wait. There's usually someone who can't wait to cut out.

Remaining in the game were two gentlemen I call Morty the Mushroom and Jabba the Gut. Morty was a small man with a crown of snow white hair and the pallor of a cadaver. The hair appeared to have been self-cut with the use of an inverted cereal bowl, a fogged mirror, and a pair of dull scissors, winding up shaped just like the top of a mushroom. His complexion, common to those who have spent most of their time spelunking, added to the impression. Jack, on the other hand, was obese past obscenity, with jowls that hung flapping like massive turkey cheeks and too many chins to count. His eyes were invisible, hidden behind puffed lids too heavy to raise past a slit.

The Shadow settled into the vacated chair to find himself across from the General, who had just switched seats with Jabba and was still giving the Mushroom hell from the previous hand. When he paused for breath he turned to Alan.

"Weak notrumps, transfers to the majors, and negative doubles," he announced, displaying his duplicate acumen. "You handle that?"

"What's two spades then?" Alan asked. "Minor suit Stayman?"

"Two spades is drop dead," the General stated.

Alan nodded. "Fine," he said. I choked back a giggle.

"O, yeah," the General added, "we play Chicago. Four deals, then we switch."

"Who's vulnerable second and third?" Alan asked.

"Dealer, of course. When the hell has it ever been otherwise?"

"Around here, I haven't any idea," Alan added a smile for the General's benefit. You'd have to know him to be aware that was the smile he presented when he was unsheathing his rapier. I settled expectantly into my chair as Jabba cut the deck with hands so bloated that for a moment the cards disappeared. When they returned Alan began to deal, presenting himself with as average a hand as you can get: ♠AKx ♡K8x ◇T98x ♣8xx. He and the Mushroom passed, the General opened with one club, Jabba belched out a spade overcall and Alan's one no trump bought the hand. The Mushroom immediately flipped the deuce of diamonds on the table.

♠	A K x		♠	Q x x x
♡	K 8 x		♡	A Q x
◇	T 9 8 x		◇	x
♣	8 x x		♣	Q J T 9 x

Not much to the hand, but Alan demonstrated some good table feel. Jabba won the diamond ace and returned the three, the Mushroom topping the ten with the queen and shifting to the ten of hearts. Alan won the ace and led the club queen, which held after the Mushroom played low with just the slightest flicker. So Alan led a spade to his king and followed with a small club. The pressure was too much for the Mushroom. Having started with king third, and now down to king and one, he thought Alan had started with ace third and was now putting it to him. He flew with the king and Jabba disgustingly slammed his ace over it. They managed to cash their two diamonds, but the overtrick had set the tone.

The next hand saw Jabba and the Mushroom score an easy partial of their own in three diamonds, so the Shadow found himself vulnerable with forty against sixty when he picked up: ♠AKJxx ♡- ◇AKQxx ♣Jxx. The General was still sorting his cards when Jabba opened with a pass out of turn.

"It's my bid!" the General roared.

"I accept the pass," said Alan. "One spade."

Mushroom passed and the General surveyed his hand. He looked pointedly down at the scoresheet, back to his hand, the scoresheet *again*, then the ceiling, pursing his lips. "Two spades," he said finally.

Alan had an ethical slam try opposite anything, so he bid three diamonds, sending the General back into his act. After some more lip-pursing and ceiling consulting he *boomed* out FOUR spades. Alan shrugged and passed. The General glared at Alan as he tabled: ♠xxxx ♡AKx ◇Txxx ♣Ax! The spade queen was third offside so Alan made only six.

"Why the hell didn't you bid over four spades?" the General demanded, his shiny pate turning pink.

"Because a quiet cuebid would have been louder than *FOUR* spades," Alan answered. The General spluttered. Jabba and the Mushroom snickered. It had been a long time since anyone had had the last word with the General. And from another golfer, yet.

Jabba dealt the last hand, this time passing in turn. Alan, holding: ♠A98xx ♡KJ7xxx ◇x ♣x also passed. The Mushroom rapped his knuckles twice on the table and looked expectantly at the General.

"One no trump!" he bellowed. Must be a bad fifteen, I thought unfairly. After all, it *could* be a great fourteen. Alan naturally trotted out Stayman. The Mushroom doubled.

"Two no trump!" the General reemphasised. Yup. I was right. And maybe he doesn't even have a major. Alan thought about it. Gang splinters aren't the easiest of hands to bid even with an expert partner. He knew he should just barrel out four hearts, but the General could have three good spades and two hearts, and the hand might play better in black, so he bid only *three* hearts, perfectly aware that sex in spacesuits would be an everyday occurrence before the General passed him there.

"Three no trump!" A little louder this time. Jabba and the Mushroom snickered. A few heads turned at adjacent tables. Alan considered the hand further. Certainly the General had three spades now, but four hearts was still the prudent call. The General probably didn't have it in him to deduce Alan's 5-6 majors and call four spades himself, protecting whatever minor tenaces he may own. But for some reason prudence did not appeal to Alan. He bid four spades.

"Four no trump!!" The General smashed his hand face down on the table. The other games stopped completely. Two kibitzers deserted their posts and drifted over. I glanced at Alan and caught a quiet smile at the corner of his mouth. Four no is *always* blackberries is these kinds of games, I remembered him saying once. He bid five diamonds. The Mushroom doubled this as well and the General came close to apoplexy.

"Five no trump!!! What the hell's the matter with you?!" he screamed, now totally out of control. Both the new kibitzers and the Mushroom hastened to calm him. When some order had been reestablished Jabba decided to get into the act with a double of his own. Alan maintained consistency and showed his king, bidding six diamonds. The Mushroom doubled in tempo and the General fought to maintain his decorum, such as it was.

"Redouble!" he sneered, apparently figuring that if he bid no trump again Alan would interpret it as a queen ask. This was corrected to six hearts by Alan and promptly doubled by the Mushroom.

"Redouble!" crowed the General, one more time. "And I hope it teaches you a damn lesson!"

By this time players had stopped their own games to partake of the action at the General's table. They grouped themselves in a circle at a respectful distance of three or four inches.

The Mushroom led the queen of clubs and the General put down his dummy, thumbing each suit into the felt as he glared at Alan.

"*Thank* you, partner," Alan cooed. "What a *beautiful* dummy. I'll do the best I can."

"See if it's better than no trumps," the General sneered.

"O, it's definitely better than no trumps," Alan smiled.

This was the entire hand:

GENERAL
♠ K T
♡ Q 9 8
♢ A J T 9 x
♣ A x x

MUSHROOM
♠ x x
♡ A
♢ K x x x
♣ Q J T x x x

JABBA THE GUT
♠ Q J x x
♡ T x x
♢ Q x x
♣ K x x

♠ A 9 8 x x
♡ K J 7 x x x
♢ x
♣ x

SHADOW DANCING

There wasn't much to the play. Alan had a merry time crossruffing and soon stroked up his gargantuan plus.

"Three no's down two on the club lead," Alan said. "Of course Blackwood and the Grand Slam Invite will be down a little more."

Shock and chagrin shook even the General, who remained, for him, curiously silent.

"Morty," barked Jabba, taking a page from the General's book, "why didn't you lead the ace of hearts?"

"Then I set up my long spade," Alan said. "There's no beat."

The spectators drifted away in amusement. The General switched seats with the Mushroom and began dealing the second round. I switched as well, placing myself in what promised to be the entertainment corner between the General and his Shadow.

I wasn't wrong, and I didn't have long to wait. This was the first hand:

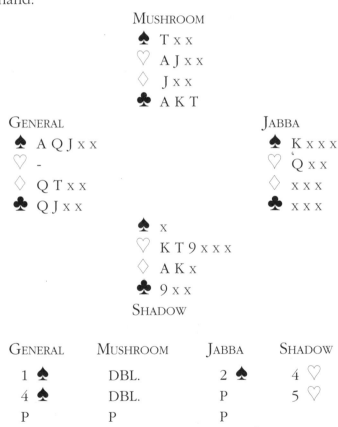

MUSHROOM
- ♠ T x x
- ♡ A J x x
- ◇ J x x
- ♣ A K T

GENERAL
- ♠ A Q J x x
- ♡ -
- ◇ Q T x x
- ♣ Q J x x

JABBA
- ♠ K x x x
- ♡ Q x x
- ◇ x x x
- ♣ x x x

SHADOW
- ♠ x
- ♡ K T 9 x x x
- ◇ A K x
- ♣ 9 x x

GENERAL	MUSHROOM	JABBA	SHADOW
1 ♠	DBL.	2 ♠	4 ♡
4 ♠	DBL.	P	5 ♡
P	P	P	

The General led the ace of spades and followed with the queen. Alan pitched a diamond. Scratching his ear, the General came a third spade. Alan ruffed, led a heart to dummy's ace as the General threw a spade, and finessed the jack through Jabba.

Another trump, the club ace, and a run of red winners squeezed the General in the minors.

"I was squeezed," he said to Jabba apologetically. Just like the General. Apologise when there's nothing he could do about it and incriminate when there is.

"Say, you can play more than golf," Morty said to Alan, and he dealt the following hand:

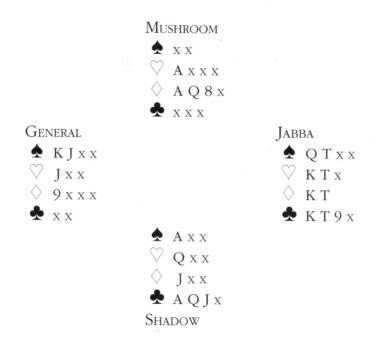

MUSHROOM
♠ x x
♡ A x x x
◇ A Q 8 x
♣ x x x

GENERAL
♠ K J x x
♡ J x x
◇ 9 x x x
♣ x x

JABBA
♠ Q T x x
♡ K T x
◇ K T
♣ K T 9 x

♠ A x x
♡ Q x x
◇ J x x
♣ A Q J x
SHADOW

The Mushroom and Jabba passed, and Alan realised he had forgotten to ask the Mushroom whether he played weak or strong no trumps. Deciding in favour of prudence he opened with one club and rebid one no trump over the Mushroom's response of one diamond. The Mushroom invited with two no trump and Alan graciously accepted. The General led the deuce of spades and Alan was relieved to see he had guessed right.

He won the third round of spades and hooked the queen of diamonds. Jabba pounced on it and led his last spade, won by the General who switched to a heart. Prospects were not good. Jabba was edging forward in his chair, unconsciously advertising the monarch. Alan rose with the ace and hooked a club.

When that won he cashed the diamond jack, noting the ten from Jabba, and hooked the diamond eight, much to the General's undisguised disgust. The ace of diamonds pinched Jabba in the rounds.

"This time *I* got squeezed!" Jabba harumphed.

"Sorry," Alan said. "No malice aforethought."

"Two in a row," chirped the Mushroom. "Like back to back birdies."

Jabba dealt the third hand, his gut rumbling menacingly as he leaned forward. The General was grimly silent. Alan picked up his hand, no doubt wishing weak two bids were part of the country club repertoire: ♠K87xxx ♡Qx ◇T ♣J9xx. Jabba and Alan passed, and the General opened one spade! Perhaps Alan wasn't quite so unhappy about not having weak two's in the arsenal anymore. The Mushroom overcalled with two diamonds and Jabba checked in with two hearts. After another pass by Alan the General bid game in hearts, sending the Mushroom into the tank. The General began to fidget.

"Whatever you're going to do, Morty, hurry up and do it, damn it! I'm not getting any younger watching you flip coins."

"Four no trump!" said the Mushroom defiantly.

Alan had little problem with that one. Whether Blackwood or Unusual his response was identical. The General doubled in his normal tone. If he'd have had a bidding box there would have been a half dozen red cards on the table. The Mushroom redoubled, and after some hesitation by the General wondering where the Mushroom had ever found the nerve to redouble him, Alan became declarer for the fifth hand in a row.

There's nothing like sitting in the right kibitzer's seat.

The General grimly led the deuce of hearts, and the Mushroom put the dummy down with an apology.

"I should have just bid five diamonds," he said. "I didn't mean to redouble."

"That's okay, partner," Alan consoled. "We're not hot."

The General looked at Alan and smiled the sort of smile Sylvester would pass a cornered Tweety Bird. It disappeared when the dummy hit with the trump tenace unexpectedly behind the General. This was the hand:

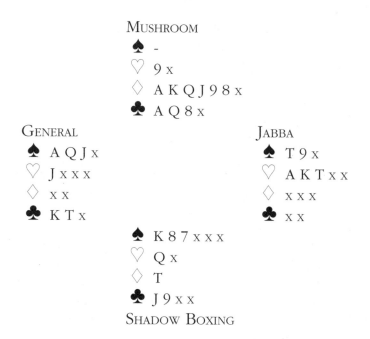

MUSHROOM
♠ -
♡ 9 x
♢ A K Q J 9 8 x
♣ A Q 8 x

GENERAL
♠ A Q J x
♡ J x x x
♢ x x
♣ K T x

JABBA
♠ T 9 x
♡ A K T x x
♢ x x x
♣ x x

♠ K 8 7 x x x
♡ Q x
♢ T
♣ J 9 x x

SHADOW BOXING

Jabba won the heart ace and king and switched to the ten of spades, pumping the dummy. Alan played a diamond to the ten and offered the jack of clubs to the General, who covered with the king. Alan won the ace and followed with the ace of diamonds, which he ruffed in hand with the Curse of Ireland. A club to the eight and the hand was all over.

"No squeeze that time," Alan said to the Mushroom. "But it's a good thing you didn't bid five diamonds. It goes set."

The General bounced his cards off the table in disgust, then had to lean down to pick them up, since it was apparent nobody was going to perform that service for him.

"What does that add up to?" the Mushroom asked.

Alan dealt the last hand, giving himself another average collection: ♠T8xx ♡Kx ♢KQJx ♣J9x. He and the General passed, the Mushroom opened with one club, and Jabba overcalled one spade. Alan bid one no trump and the General bid a forceful two spades, which rode back to Alan.

Pass, I thought.

"Double"(!), he said, and after three passes led the king of diamonds.

GENERAL DUMMY

♠ J 9 x
♡ A x x x
◇ x x x
♣ x x x

SHADOW CLUBBING

♣ T 8 x x
♡ K x
◇ K Q J x
♣ J 9 x

The king of diamonds held. Alan continued with the queen, and that held. He led his low diamond to the Mushroom's ace, also holding. The Mushroom promptly cashed the ace and king of clubs, the second of which caught Jabba's queen, and led a third round. When Jabba went into thought, book already in the defensive bank, the General began to fume. Jabba finally ditched a heart, Alan winning the jack. The General emitted a demonstrative 'Bah!', like the brief protestation of a violated sheep.

Then Alan went into thought for a moment or two. He fingered the heart king, but instead put a small spade on the table. Jabba played low, and the queen appeared from the Mushroom. Jabba won the king and finessed the spade nine. When it held, Mushroom pitching a club, he cashed the spade jack and followed with the ace of hearts. Alan unblocked the king! The Mushroom won the ensuing heart with the queen and the spade ten was soon promoted to the third undertrick.

Eight hundred in the glue. Only two dollars, but what value could be placed on watching the General jump to his feet so quickly his chair flipped backwards to land with a loud thud on the floor? What price attached to the sound of unprintable yelping, the sight of cards like giant gnats flying across the room? A king's ransom could not cover the giggles of the club members as the General stormed out.

When order was restored Jabba and the Mushroom invited

me to fill in, but Alan told them he had a plane to catch, and after a few more handshakes we were on our way to the parking lot.

"The General got what he deserved for that manure-laced raise," I said, "but how'd you know to double? It should have come from the Mushroom's side."

"The General told me."

"Eh? How's that?"

"He bid it a little *too* forcefully, even for him."

I looked at the Shadow. "You remember that psyche class we took from Zany Pylyshyn?"

"Who could forget? ...And in answer to your next question, yeah, I aced it."

Shadow
Meets the Feminist

TRUE TO HIS NATURE, THE SHADOW slipped into the Toronto Nationals virtually unnoticed. Arriving in the city on unrelated family business, he found himself with a free day and an urge to play. A telephone call to one of my erstwhile wives ferreted out that I was indeed in town for the tournament, and like the slink he is Alan used the information to sneak up on me yet again. This time he found me sitting crosslegged under a tree on a grassy harbourside knoll with my guitar at my side and a tube steak halfway to my mouth.

"Greetings, earthling," the gravelled voice behind me spoke. Startled, and unable to recognise the disguised croak, I whirled to find the grinning face of the Shadow in the shadow of the tree.

"Alan! Jeez, I could've choked!"

"Only if I'd waited another second until you had that howitzer in your mouth."

"Siddown, siddown. How'd you find me?"

"Roslyn told me you were in town; I ran into 'Da Canooz' in the lobby. He guessed you'd be out here." He threw his jacket on the grass beside me and settled himself as I went on filling my face. "Wanna play?"

"What, today?" I mumbled. "In the Swiss?"

"Yep."

"Your timing couldn't be worse. I just agreed to play with a friend."

"Got another pair?"

"Two of them; we're a six-bagger."

"Too bad. Your friend be upset if you bow out, maybe play another time with him? I don't mean to push, Mikey. Only if it would be cool for him and if he got another partner. Just that today's my only day; I fly tomorrow morning."

I shrugged. "Sorry, bud. Nothing I'd like more, but it won't wash. I can leave the team at the break,'though. We can have dinner at a nice little upstairs oyster bar I know, not too far from here."

"Sold. I'm going to head inside, then. See if I can scare something up." He stood, giving his jacket a quick brush with his palm. "Later."

Still chewing, I waved.

*   *   *

A few hours later, after two wins and a loss, I had talked our teammates into letting my partner and me sit out matches four and five. That not only set up a five hour break, but enabled me to search out the Shadow and kibitz his last match before we headed for dinner. He was already seated and shuffling cards when I pulled up a chair beside him. His opponents had yet to arrive at the table.

"Howzit?" I asked.

"We won the first two in dull blitzes. The last match I don't wish to discuss." I snuck a glance over the top edge of my glasses at Alan's partner, an Ontario player of decent ability, but one certainly given to flights of fancy. His eyes remained down, glued to the deck he was shuffling in a deliberate manner.

"I see," I saw, and said.

A few minutes later, all four boards at the table having been made, the Shadow's opponents made their tardy appearance. It was soon apparent that their timing was intentional, a result not of traditional lineups in the ladies' room between matches, but the seminal thrust of gamesmanship, intended to annoy and hopefully to distract.

They were thirty-something what I presumed to be ladies. So much for presumption.

"Afternoon, ladies," Alan said pleasantly. Righty gave Alan a curt nod as she seated herself. She was as plain and average looking a person as one could imagine, the kind Alice Sheldon had dubbed 'the women men don't see'. There was not a single feature about her or her clothing that stood out, the only unique thing being that absolutely nothing was unique.

Lefty, on the other hand, was quite another matter.

"These made?" were her first words, indicating the boards with a glower as she settled her bulk into her chair.

"They are," Alan said, still with a smile.

"Then we'll make them again," she said, tossing her partner a board and pulling out the cards of another. Gameswomanship thrust number two. She began to shuffle, ignoring Alan and his partner. They gave each other a glance, then took out the remaining two hands to redeal them. In all the time I'd played bridge, I'd only once before seen anyone insinuate that unfair advantage had been taken in a 'pre-shuffle'. In effect, this woman had called Alan and his partner cheaters. This bovine, muu-muu clad blob of human protoplasm, this mean, porcine-featured, pepper and salt witch-wiry haired hog of a bridge player had had the audacity to insinuate that one of the ACBL's well-known lights was worse than unethical.

The Shadow's smile was no longer in evidence. I tightened my seat belt.

Alan gave his deck a few quick and expert shuffles, then placed it before Ms. Blandness on his right.

"Cut, please," he said, and smiled. Shadow thrust number one. Mimicking Alan, his partner placed *his* shuffled deck before Miz Bovinity. She angrily rapped a knuckle on top of it and at that moment happened to look up and make eye contact with me. I had the instant impression that were we ever to be stranded together on a deserted island her first desire would be to use me as food. As a kibitzer I had no desire to be barred, for any non-reason, so with pokerface in place I preempted her.

"Anyone like a water, or coffee," I said, standing. "On me." I smiled at the 'ladies' as I edged away from the table. Grunting, Her Largesse shook her head.

"Thanks, black," Alan's partner said.

It didn't take me long, and I returned just as they were finishing the first hand.

"No swing," Alan said to me as I passed a coffee to his partner.

"Well, there might have been," Her Bovinity divined, "if your partner had only invited, as he should have." Thrust three, and a particularly unpleasant one, being that of handing an opponent an unsolicited lesson.

Alan's right temple pulsed as his jaw tightened. I saw him take a slow breath.

"My partner is aware I seldom refuse an invitation," he said. "Neither when I have a non-minimum, nor against weak defenders." Shadow thrust number two.

The next three boards were flat as a politician's promises, clear pushes with perhaps an overtrick IMP swung one way or another here or there.

"Caddy!" Alan held up a hand for the boards to be exchanged. "Those were four dull hands," he said. "Maybe we should've ghoulied them instead of reshuffling." Shadow thrust three. I hoped the last three hands would have some entertainment in them.

It wasn't to be. Hand five was as flat as the four previous, and hand six had the 'ladies' congratulating themselves on staying out of a diamond slam at which they'd never even sniffed, playing three no trump with two overtricks.

"I guess your boys will be in that one," Miz Bovinity gloated, the snips and snaps of gamespersonship continuing to ping-pong back and forth.

And so it came to the last board. Nobody vulnerable, the Shadow in second seat, down a swing with all aware of it.

That was when he picked up the Curses of England, Ireland, Scotland, and Wales, in the form of:

♠ T 9 x ♡ A K 9 x ♢ 9 8 x ♣ T 9 x

I could see the gears grind in the Shadow's mind. What to do? Psyche a one heart opener, or perhaps a weak two hearts? Were the vulnerability favourable even a three heart shot would not be unreasonable.

All these thoughts were quickly put to rest when Miz Invisible announced a skip bid and placed the 3♡ card on the table herself!

Alan had little doubt what to do now. After his pass Miz Bovinity hesitated briefly, then bid four hearts! With but a moment to lick his mental chops, he saw his partner place the 4♠ card down, and the match appeared lost to what would surely be another push.

Except when the auction went around to Miz Bovinity she pulled out the red 'double' card and thumbed it onto the table.

Later Alan told me that at this point he mentally rolled his eyes skyward to thank the card gods. When the auction came around to him once again he pulled out the blue 'redouble' card. Miz Bovinity took a solid ten second look at it, then pulled the green 'pass' card out, a sneer decorating the upper right corner of her lip.

The heart queen was led and Alan tabled the dummy. "I hope two pitches do you some good, pard," he said.

And to his amazement his partner followed to the trick!

This was the entire hand:

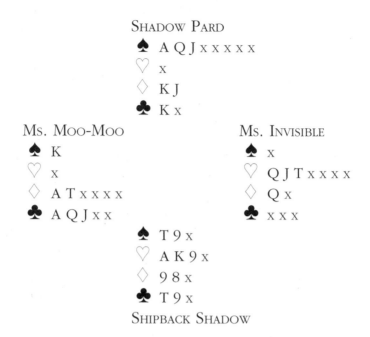

Shadow Pard
- ♠ A Q J x x x x x
- ♡ x
- ◇ K J
- ♣ K x

Ms. Moo-Moo
- ♠ K
- ♡ x
- ◇ A T x x x x
- ♣ A Q J x x

Ms. Invisible
- ♠ x
- ♡ Q J T x x x x
- ◇ Q x
- ♣ x x x

- ♠ T 9 x
- ♡ A K 9 x
- ◇ 9 8 x
- ♣ T 9 x

Shipback Shadow

Alan's partner won the ace and led a small spade. When the king appeared there were two dummy entries. He led a spade to the Curse of Wales and delayed his pitch, calling for the Curse of Scotland. Miz Moo was having none of that. If she had ducked he would have won the king, entered dummy with the spade ten, ditched the diamond jack, and led the Curse of Ireland up for the second overtrick. Instead they cashed their aces and got the hell out of there.

Plus ten-eighty; win eleven IMPs; tie the match!

* * *

Half an hour later the Shadow and I were squirting lemon juice over oysters on the half-shell and dipping homemade bread into passable clam chowder. We had avoided bridge talk during the walk over to catch up on personal news, waiting until we were settled with the edge of hunger dulled.

Finally I could stand it no longer. "How the hell did you know she was going to sit for the redouble?" I asked.

"Elementary, my dear Mikey," Alan said, "if you know the difference between a feminist woman and a liberated woman."

"Is this a joke?"

"May be. But the answer's crucial to the hand."

"Do tell."

"'A feminist woman wants to have *cohones*; a liberated woman just wants them to hang on her wall as trophies."

I had to laugh. "So this was a feminist?"

"Capital Eff. She's got *cohones*. There was no way she was going to get stampeded by a lowly *man!*"

"Ri-ight,"

"And in my opinion she was wearing four-pounders. She *did* go for throat raising to four hearts on a stiff!"

"This is a hand Zee would love."

"Feel free to pass it his way," the Shadow said. "Now how about another plate of these oysters and a beer and damn the entree? You might get to meet Miz Moo in the evening session!"

Shadow Loose in White Rock

IT WAS SHORTLY AFTER FIVE AYEM ON the Ides of April. The Shadow thought that would be a fine time to see how many rings it took to get me to the phone.

"This better be good," I grunted into the mouthpiece.

"Only two rings," the phone spoke back, "You must have been getting ready to wake up anyway."

"I spend hours getting ready. Who the hell is this?"

"Mikey, you jerk; you wound me."

"Alan!"

"Get out of bed, there's a beaut of a sunrise on the way."

I sat up. "Where are you?"

"About three hundred klicks southwest and on a glide path. Wanna pick me up?"

I lay down. "Sure. See you at noon."

"I'll cab it. See you around seven." Click.

I was asleep again in seconds.

Somewhere past seven the dogs, apparently unaware the door buzzer was already insisting I rise, informed me a Shadow was on the front step. Viewing the world with more jaundice than clarity I threw on a robe, demanded Furface and Troglodog shut their yaps, and stumbled down two flights to open the door.

"Greetings," Alan said, stepping inside while raising an eyebrow at the tousled remains of my hair. "I can see coffee's not ready. I won't ask you to carry a bag." I followed him up the stairs as the dogs went through their sniff and greet routine.

"I'll grind some Kona beans. I presume you're coming from home?"

"I am indeed. I can see Pooh Bear hasn't changed." The Bouncing Bichon was in the middle of her pogo act. "Who's the other one?"

"Formerly my sister's dog, Snowball. I usually call her Furface, now. The dog; not my sister." The little Bichon was poised on her hind legs, a furry albino ballerina, fanning the air with her two front paws cupped together. "I adopted her. Bear I've renamed Troglodog. I think she's infectious; if you spend more than an hour around her your I.Q. drops by fifty points."

"Helluva view, Mikey."

"You should see it from upstairs. Like yours minus the palm trees. I'm glad you finally made it here. How long you staying? More than an hour, I hope?"

"I've got two days, but if I start feeling stupid during coffee I'll be on my way."

"You sleep on the plane?"

"Most of the way. I'm pretty rested. Why?"

"How about if I treat you to a day in White Rock? A bistro brunch in Crescent Beach a few miles west, an espresso at the Blue Monkey, on White Rock Beach, a block down the hill. Maybe an afternoon siesta, then dinner down the hill again at the Giraffe, my favourite spot. Five star, kiddo."

"Consider my arm twisted. Sounds great."

"Not only that, but if I ask Corinne nicely she might let us start a half hour early, and we'll be in time to stroke a little blue-hair bridge at the local club. Drinking before, during, and after dinner highly recommended."

"Is this like that afternoon game we played at 'Bucky's' in Toronto?"

"Only the names have been changed. With two or three exceptions they're a lovable bunch of seniors out having a hoot."

"Sounds like great fun; I'm in. Now how about grinding that coffee?"

*   *   *

White Rock, one of the warmest and sunniest spots in all of Canada, is at its best in spring. The Shadow and I walked through a gauntlet of blazing rhododendrons as we approached the small community centre that housed the weekly duplicate of sometimes twenty tables of bantering and enthusiastic retired citizens.

Being a full ten minutes early didn't come close to securing ourselves a north-south. Most were reserved well into the twenty-first century. White Rock bridge players are nothing if not optimistic. Being just on the short side of a half century qualified me in a small handful of the club's youngest players.

We were, however, early enough for me to estimate the number of tables in play and grab an east- west where the movement, a straight Mitchell, would be sure to allow us to miss back-to-back confrontations with certain of the club regulars who had clearly been weaned on pickles.

"I've never seen anyone move so fast for an east-west," Alan said as he seated himself across from me.

"Trust me, there's good reason."

"I won't ask. Till later."

"Ask me anytime. I won't tell. Till later."

The White Rock ladies put out a nice spread of finger food and desserts for the games. Our first opponents, a pleasant lady resembling a sparrow and a taciturn fellow who last spoke the previous century, came to the table licking their fingers. Fortunately Alan and I had assumed the responsibility of shuffling the hands and dealing. There was no chance of anything sweet and sticky adhering to our cards. For one round, anyway.

"Good evening, boys," Sparrow Lady said as she seated

herself. It's so nice to be pushing fifty and still be called 'boy'. "You're new here, aren't you?" she said to Alan.

"A virgin in White Rock," he smiled.

"Honey, if you're a virgin," she cackled, patting his hand, "let me be your teacher."

"She's not kidding," her partner spoke, still licking a finger.

"Good thing I am," Alan answered.

It's amazing how often the first round of a session can set the tone for the entire game.

With both sides vulnerable I opened one club and the Taciturn Fellow overcalled one diamond, catching Alan with: ♠Ax ♡Axx ♢AJ962 ♣Kxx. He decided he would be pleased to defend and passed with the intention of sitting for a protective double from my side. Sparrow Lady, however, bid one heart, I passed, and now T.F. bid one spade. Wondering if I might have psyched on the first hand out of the box Alan decided on the cheapest of the three cue bids available to him. After his two diamond bid Sparrow Lady passed, and I was left to find a call holding: ♠Kxx ♡QTx ♢754 ♣AQJx.

Two no trump may appear an obvious call to some, but I thought my diamond stop a trifle tenuous. I decided to toss an ambicuebid back, and tried two hearts. Alan closed proceedings with a jump to three no trump. The bidding did not deter Sparrow Lady from leading fourth best from her longest and strongest.

"Thanks, Mikey; lovely dummy," Alan said. "Clever of you to insist we not play weak no trumps. Queen, please."

When the heart queen held, T.F. following small, Alan called for a small diamond. When T.F. played the three under the four Alan played the deuce under the three! Sparrow Lady played a small club and she and T.F. exchanged glances. When they looked at Alan he smiled at both of them.

"*Deep* finesse," he said.

This was the entire hand:

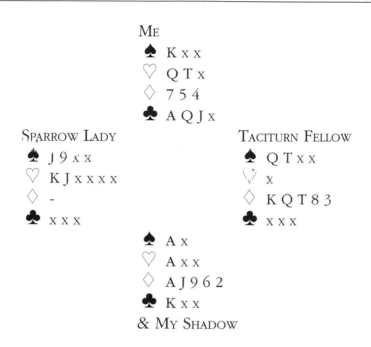

ME
♠ K x x
♡ Q T x
♢ 7 5 4
♣ A Q J x

SPARROW LADY
♠ J 9 x x
♡ K J x x x x
♢ -
♣ x x x

TACITURN FELLOW
♠ Q T x x
♡ x
♢ K Q T 8 3
♣ x x x

♠ A x
♡ A x x
♢ A J 9 6 2
♣ K x x

& MY SHADOW

Alan now called for the seven of diamonds, ducking in hand when T.F. played the queen, S.L. following with a spade. T.F. switched to a baby spade. Alan won in hand with the ace, cashed the heart ace, and followed with four rounds of clubs to produce this position:

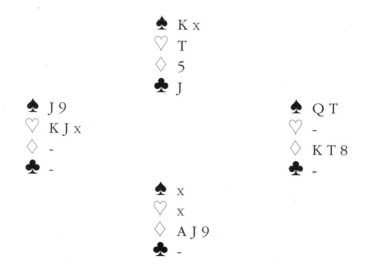

♠ K x
♡ T
♢ 5
♣ J

♠ J 9
♡ K J x
♢ -
♣ -

♠ Q T
♡ -
♢ K T 8
♣ -

♠ x
♡ x
♢ A J 9
♣ -

On the last club T.F. was forced to keep all three diamonds, and therefore bared the spade queen as Alan and the Sparrow Lady both ditched idle hearts. Now Alan took the diamond finesse as S.L. threw the heart jack, but the next diamond left her helpless and the third overtrick rolled home.

"Well stroked," I said.

"I rescind my teaching offer," Sparrow Lady chirped. "Looks aren't everything."

Then she got even.

With nobody vulnerable I started with one heart, T.F. overcalled two diamonds, and Alan doubled negatively. Holding ♠AQ765 ♡Jxxx ♢Tx ♣Jx, she stepped in fearlessly with two spades. When my three clubs and T.F.'s three diamond rebid came back to her, she *rebid* the spades! That was enough for Alan. He thought the contract would play better in 'six', so he doubled.

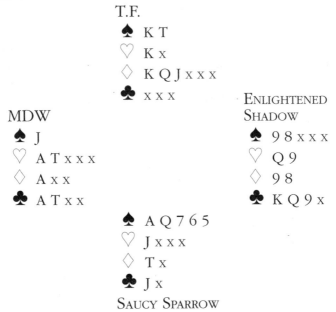

T.F.
♠ K T
♡ K x
♢ K Q J x x x
♣ x x x

MDW
♠ J
♡ A T x x x
♢ A x x
♣ A T x x

ENLIGHTENED SHADOW
♠ 9 8 x x x
♡ Q 9
♢ 9 8
♣ K Q 9 x

♠ A Q 7 6 5
♡ J x x x
♢ T x
♣ J x

SAUCY SPARROW

You'd have thought by this time Alan would be cautious when holding the four curses, realising the card gods would look much more kindly upon the Sparrow Lady than they did the Feminist.

Any black suit lead would have been a happy result for our

side, but somehow I talked myself into thinking the opponents had a four-three heart fit and it would behoove me to give Alan a series of ruffs rather than start a forcing defense. Well, I was close. After I got off to the heart ace lead we were lucky to nip the contract a trick.

"I thought I was going to make that for a minute," Sparrow Lady said.

"You'll do all right with minus a hundred," Alan said. "We can do better playing in clubs."

"Well, that's kind of you to say so; maybe I'll change my mind about you." And she patted his hand once again.

I thought it was kind of him not to comment on my lead, myself.

We had finished both hands quickly, and as the first round in White Rock is notoriously elastic we had plenty of time to get coffee and goodies from the kitchen and step outside to chat and munch and enjoy a leisurely smoke.

"Sorry about the lead," I said.

"Not to worry. It might have been worse."

"What could be worse?"

"Ace and a diamond," he teased.

"Not even in your nightmares," I shot back.

Round two was soon called, and the Yo-Yo bridge continued.

Our opponents were a stout octogenarian affectionately dubbed the Tortoise, due as much to his humpbacked shape as to his reputation as the slowest player west of the Rockies, and his regular partner, a lady with silver-blue hair and twinkling eyes and a gracious martyr with the patience of Job.

The Tortoise carried with him a stack of used convention cards at least three inches thick. Two wide elastics surrounded the pile at right angles. It was his version of a criss-cross squeeze, a testimonial badge of his experience, like a ribbon-clad retired officer at a wedding party. That the pile took up fully a third of the table space in front of him seemed not to matter. That the other two-thirds had to house a bidding box, the current convention card, some pencils, perhaps a drink and a cookie or two on a napkin was a minor inconvenience, and not just to him. Since thirteen cards were must additions to the scenario, and because he liked to put them face down on the table, picking them up slowly one at a time, like a nickel-dime poker player acting in a self-directed film, a little juggling was a physical necessity.

The Shadow and the Martyr and I had our hands sorted and memorised and were exchanging weak smiles as we waited for the Tortoise, who was keeping up a continual and habitual banter as he guided each card into his mildly arthritic left claw. Unless both hands were claimers our way at trick one there would be no smoke break after *this* round.

Finally the Tortoise's head emerged from its shell, and he opened proceedings with a game bid in hearts.

Without a doubt one of the greatest drawbacks of preemption is that it frequently goads the opponents into makeable contracts they would seldom if ever reach without the additional shove. Such was now the case, and these were our hands:

Me

♠ A J T x
♡ A x
◇ K T x x
♣ T 9 7

♠ K Q x
♡ x x
◇ A x x x
♣ A K 8 x

& My Shadow

Tortoise	MDW	Martyr	Shadow
4 ♡	P	P	DBL
P	5 ♡*	P	5NT**
P	6 ◇	P	P
DBL	6NT***	P	P
P			

*   Too good for 4♠; may as well show this on the way.

**   Pick a slam.

***   I believe you.

Once more into the breech, and testimony that at matchpoints bad bidding is frequently its own reward.

Looking at both hands it is clear that game in no trump is as high as one would like to be. This was a little hard to reach as we didn't start bidding until the four level. Perhaps there is something to be said for preemptive pushes after all, since there was no way we could have stopped in four no trump.

The Tortoise led the heart king, Alan ducking as the Martyr followed suit. On the heart queen continuation she pitched a small club. Alan cashed the spade jack and led a small spade to the queen, maintaining entry flexibility, as the Tortoise followed once and then pitched a small heart. Now Alan cashed the diamond ace to which the Martyr played the *jack* with a clearly martyred expression.

On certain other of the players in the field, such an expression would mark the presence of the anti-percentage jack. But the Martyr was as honest as she was resigned, and a diamond to the ten brought a small spade from her hand.

At this point Alan called for the Curse of Ireland, and when the Martyr followed with a baby he floated it! The Tortoise played a heart. Plus nine-ninety.

I had more than enough time to think about the hand while the Tortoise entered his score, juggled his paraphernalia, and picked up his next hand. Alan's careful curse had been a thoughtful play. Had he floated the seven, for instance, the Martyr could have covered the ensuing club, and when Alan reentered the dummy she could have *ducked* the last club, effectively locking away the long spade. The early unblock had prevented that possibility from ever happening.

"Nine may not be just the Beatles' fave number," I said.

Then the Tortoise got *his* revenge, as the bridge Yo-Yo once more changed directions.

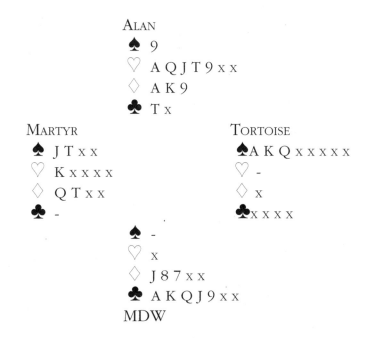

```
                     ALAN
                     ♠  9
                     ♡  A Q J T 9 x x
                     ◇  A K 9
                     ♣  T x
    MARTYR                            TORTOISE
    ♠  J T x x                        ♠ A K Q x x x x x
    ♡  K x x x x                      ♡  -
    ◇  Q T x x                        ◇  x
    ♣  -                              ♣ x x x x
                     ♠  -
                     ♡  x
                     ◇  J 8 7 x x
                     ♣  A K Q J 9 x x
                     MDW
```

With only the opponents vulnerable I started with one club, and after a pass by the Martyr and one heart by Alan the Tortoise decided to preempt us once again, this time with four spades. I brought diamonds into the picture with four no trump and the Martyr, deciding it was Blackwood, tried to disrupt communications with five spades. When Alan introduced diamonds at the six level the Tortoise thought now would be a good time to bid one more for the road. I naturally passed, and Alan could hardly be blamed for doubling.

I led a top club, and the Tortoise tortured us with a slow and interminable rounded suit crossruff, scoring up sixteen-sixty as he smothered any smoke break. Ignominy was piled on pain as the director called the move and came to our table to hurry us along.

"I was wishing I had a trump to lead," I said as we stood. "I guess I had to lead a diamond to you so you could switch to the trump."

"Doesn't help. He ruffs diamonds instead of hearts and sets up the queen for a pitch. This time the nines got *us*. We had to switch our black nines and you had to not lead yours even if you had it!"

Two more rounds saw a string of average results, and a smoke break called by the director. Outside the sun had set and a mild spring chill was in the air.

"Beautiful evening," Alan said.

"Say, don't I know you?" One of the club regulars, a fellow in his late fifties who dabbled regularly both at the track and in a jar of Grecian Formula, stepped from the shadows at the far end of the porch and approached Alan. The stub of a thick and cheap cigar sat clamped in the corner of his mouth.

"I don't think so. I'm (censored)," Alan said, sticking out his right hand.

"Doesn't ring a bell," the fellow said, knitting his brows as he extracted the cigar with his left hand while taking Alan's hand with his right. "Thought maybe we met somewhere else."

"Maybe at the regional in Victoria last year," Alan suggested. "That was the last time I was in B.C."

"Naw. Seems to me it was bowling somewhere. You a bowler?"

I could see the wheels spinning swiftly in Alan's mind. What's better, a total lie, or a partial truth? I, of course, was prepared to go in whatever direction he chose.

Sizing up the fellow as a man who was certain what he has seen, Alan decided not to try to bluff his way through.

"I've bowled before, but not often. You mean five pins or ten?"

"Ten. You a southpaw? I think I saw you blow a perfect game in Salt Lake once. Brooklyned your last ball."

Alan smiled. "I'm a righty," he said. Not a total lie; he *is* ambidextrous with most things.

"Coulda sworn," the fellow said, shaking his head. He drifted back to the far end of the porch.

"Well?" I said quietly when he was out of earshot.

"Well, I remember *him*. The sunnavabitch booed and flashed me the 'choke' sign."

"Don't you wear that big 'stache when you're bowling?"

"Yeah," Alan shrugged, "but I glared at him. We made solid eye contact."

"When was this?" I asked as we headed back inside.

"Fifteen, sixteen years." He shrugged again and smiled at me.

As we approached and I saw who our next opponents were I stopped Alan and whispered quickly in his ear, "Strike negative doubles except over preempts; this round only."

Third shrug in thirty seconds. "Okay." And we sat down against a pair of old tigers with a propensity to overcall suits as good as nine or ten fourth, and not just at the one level. Vulnerability, of course, was for children.

"Gentlemen..." Alan said as we sat down.

"Is that the singular or the plural?" the long-toothed tiger in the north seat said. "If the former I want to know which of us you're referring to."

Alan smiled and removed his cards from the board.

"That wasn't a rhetorical question," L.T. Tiger pressed.

"In that case make it singular," Alan said. "And you can guess from there."

The short-toothed tiger in the south seat snickered. Nothing like a friendly start to a round.

With only the tigers vulnerable Long Tooth skipped the bidding with two spades, Alan passed, and Short Tooth raised to three spades, catching me with: ♠- ♡Qx ◇AQTx ♣AKQJxxx. My mouth working faster than my mind, not an unusual occurrence, I bid six clubs in tempo. Short Tooth thought it would play better in twelve, and Long Tooth led the spade queen, not thinking S.T.'s double might have Lightneresque connotations.

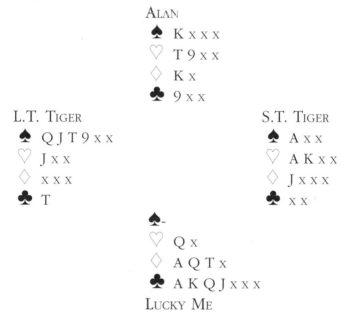

ALAN
♠ K x x x
♡ T 9 x x
◇ K x
♣ 9 x x

L.T. TIGER
♠ Q J T 9 x x
♡ J x x
◇ x x x
♣ T

S.T. TIGER
♠ A x x
♡ A K x x
◇ J x x x
♣ x x

♠-
♡ Q x
◇ A Q T x
♣ A K Q J x x x

LUCKY ME

The play took only seconds. Three ruffs in hand, one of them with an honour, set up the spade king for a pitch. I had drawn one round of trumps along the way and used the Curse of Ireland as my final entry, drawing the last trump in the process. Long Tooth was livid.

"That was no damn Lightner double ," he barked. "Dummy hasn't bid a suit!"

"And what were you leading if I hadn't doubled?" S.T. asked reasonably. "How many matchpoints do you think we were getting for six clubs undoubled?"

Needless to say, Long Tooth was floundering in waters too deep to formulate an answer.

"Was that a rhetorical question?" Alan asked sweetly, pulling his next hand out.

This time the colours were switched, me and my Shadow at unfavourable. Two passes came to my: ♠AQJxx ♡K8xx ♢xx ♣xx. I started with one spade, L.T. overcalled two clubs, pass from Alan, and two diamonds from S.T. which was passed back to the Shadow. He doubled, and I alerted.

"What the hell is that?" S.T. asked.

"Just an urge to compete," I said. "He didn't have a negative double available to him at his last turn."

"Then why do you have them on your cards?" L.T. piped in, pointing at our conventions. "Director!" he screamed.

Finn, the tireless commander of both the White Rock and Tsawassen duplicates, appeared at our side. After being brought up to date he asked me to answer L.T.'s question.

"I would have before if he'd waited for an answer instead of screaming to interrupt you." Tough to resist editorialising. "Since I'm familiar with their overcalling style we decided to dump them just for this round. If we hadn't I wouldn't have alerted the double of two diamonds; it'd be for blood."

Satisfied, Finn told us to play on.

S.T. passed, and not thinking my hand too suitable for defense I tried two hearts. L.T. was right there with three clubs. Alan tried another double.

"And what the hell is that one?" S.T. asked.

"Did I alert?" I retorted.

Everybody passed and Alan led the eight of spades.

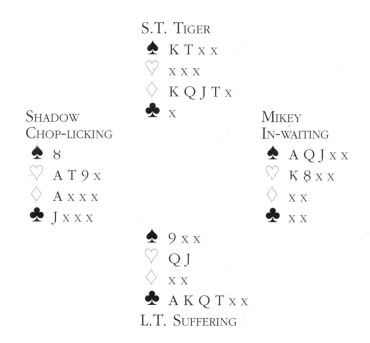

S.T. TIGER
♠ K T x x
♡ x x x
♢ K Q J T x
♣ x

SHADOW
CHOP-LICKING
♠ 8
♡ A T 9 x
♢ A x x x
♣ J x x x

MIKEY
IN-WAITING
♠ A Q J x x
♡ K 8 x x
♢ x x
♣ x x

♠ 9 x x
♡ Q J
♢ x x
♣ A K Q T x x
L.T. SUFFERING

Granted we could make a lot of hearts, due to the fortuitous lie of the cards. But who cared? After two spades and a spade ruff Alan cashed the heart ace, then the diamond ace, and led the heart ten to my king. I placed another spade on the table and the club jack was promoted for the third undertrick. Long Tooth's lividity had increased with the turn of each card. When it came time to enter the score he was positively pallid.

"We can kiss *this* game goodbye," Short Tooth said acidly.

"Too bad," Alan rubbed, signing the scorecard and rising from the table. "We didn't need the good scores; everybody else has been drilling us."

Back outside I turned to Alan. "With one exception, and we don't get to play her, it couldn't have happened to a nicer pair."

"Glad to be of assistance. I presume negative doubles are back on?"

"I presume that's rhetorical?"

Alan chuckled.

Little happened for the next few rounds, an exception being when one of the club's more charming senior citizens asked Alan to autograph her scorecard. Regretfully the card gods chose to reward her with a zero when Alan and I easily bid to a grand slam simply because we were playing the Blue Team Two Diamond, one of his favourite toys. Our hands were: ♠AKxx ♡AKxx ◇QJxx ♣x sitting opposite ♠xx ♡QJxxx ◇AKxx ♣Ax.

Just before the last round the Shadow slipped to the biffy, and I took the opportunity to go outside for a short walk down the garden path, so to speak. When I returned I found Alan already at the table, and sitting down to take the north seat was none other than Grecian Formula.

"I'm telling you," G.F. was saying, "I never..."

"Forget a face?" Alan finished. "Well, it must have been somewhere, then."

"You been to Albuquerque?"

"One night only, and I spent it all at Red Dog Dan's."

"How about Santa Fe?"

"Only passing through."

"Dammit, I *know* it was somewhere in that part of the country. Quite a while back, too."

"Well, don't let it ruin your concentration for bridge," Alan directed, pulling out his cards. "We can try to figure it out after the game. You ever have lighter hair?"

G.F.'s partner was a slim squirrelly fellow I had never seen before. Perhaps five feet and change standing up he looked almost childlike scrunched in his chair. His small nose twitched as he nervously pursed and unpursed his thin lips, examining his cards like a rodent on a limb with an acorn in its paws.

"This guy's a pro," Squirrel told G.F. "Aintcha seen his picture in the 'Bulletin'? C'mon, you're up."

"Well, maybe that's it," G.F. acquiesced, his attention turning to his hand, which was: ♠T98xxx ♡T8xx ◇QJ ♣x. In a few moments he found himself on lead against a small slam on this auction:

G.F.	MDW	SQUIRREL	SHADOW
P	1 ♣	P	1 ◇
P	1NT	P	2 ♣* (CHECKBACK)
P	2 ◇	P	2 ♡
P	3 ♣	P	6 ◇
P	P	P	

Reasoning that the Squirrel would have doubled had he a black suit void or the club ace G.F. narrowed his choices quickly down to something red. On the auction a heart was as unappealing as the deceptive diamond jack was attractive. He thumbed it onto the table.

This was the entire hand:

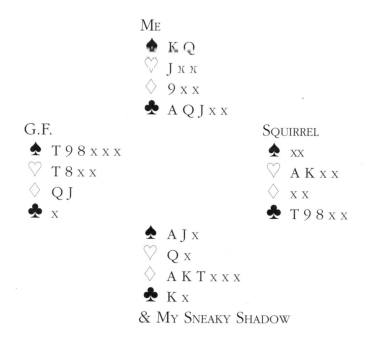

ME
♠ K Q
♡ J x x
♢ 9 x x
♣ A Q J x x

G.F.
♠ T 9 8 x x x
♡ T 8 x x
♢ Q J
♣ x

SQUIRREL
♠ x x
♡ A K x x
♢ x x
♣ T 9 8 x x

♠ A J x
♡ Q x
♢ A K T x x x
♣ K x

& MY SNEAKY SHADOW

It seemed that Alan hardly thought about it. He won the opening lead and put the other top diamond on the table.

"Nine never," he said as the queen plopped.

The last board was anticlimactic, the most prosaic of averages. The players were quickly forming a huddle around the computer, waiting for the first scores to emerge. Alan saw G.F. bent over Finn's shoulder.

"Let's get out of here," he said, pulling me by the elbow. "I don't feel like waiting for his memory to get jogged."

"What was that 'nine never' drivel on the first hand? How did you know not to take the hook?"

"Because he's the kind of guy who makes a decision and then acts on it *demonstratively*. When he decided to jeer me when I blew my perfect game, he did it loud enough to make an ass of himself; when he decided to colour his hair, he went all the way with boot black; and when he decided to lead the diamond, he *thumbed* it into the table. I figured him as a guy who overdoes everything. By the way, you might have owned the queen of diamonds instead of the queen of spades. That was quite a preference you took."

"Thanks, I'll take that as a compliment even though you don't mean it. I *did* have the Curse of Scotland. If the nine's good enough for Reese to write a treatise on, it's good enough for me to evaluate a hand on. Nice two heart call, also by the way."

Shortly thereafter we sat under the stars on my top deck, brandies in hand to ward the night chill. The lights of Blaine, Washington twinkled to the southeast, two klicks across Semiahmoo Bay; Victoria glowed weakly on the southern horizon, to the west Tsawassen shone across Boundary Bay, and below us White Rock curved like a serpent toward Crescent Beach.

"This is a two hundred and seventy degree view to forever, Mikey. I can see why you're happy here."

"I think it's the best spot in the country, much as you live in what I think is the best spot in yours. The difference, you'll note, is that I've visited Maui half a dozen times and this is your first stop in White Rock."

"The difference is palm trees..."

"...Being able to go out at night in a tank top and a tee shirt, all year 'round..."

"...Wahinis in bikinis..."

"...Fresh fruit, and fish..."

"...Fresh ladies..."

"...Prime pakalolo..."

"...Prime feminine pulchritude..."

"I think Troglodog is beginning to have an effect on you..."

And the night wound on until, brandy depleted, we faded into its shadows.